LA BELLE CAPTIVE

LA BELLE CAPTIVE

a novel

ALAIN ROBBE-GRILLET

RENÉ MAGRITTE

Translated and with an Essay by Ben Stoltzfus

UNIVERSITY OF CALIFORNIA PRESS   BERKELEY   LOS ANGELES   LONDON

La Belle Captive was originally published in French by La Bibliothèque des Arts, Lausanne and Paris, © 1975 Cosmos Textes, Brussels; translated by permission of Alain Robbe-Grillet and the Georges Borchardt Literary Agency.

University of California Press
Berkeley and Los Angeles, California

University of California Press, Ltd.
London, England

Plates 1–77 are reproduced from the original French novel. Figs. 1, 3, 6, 14, 16, and 18 are reproduced from Suzi Gablik, *Magritte* (London: Thames and Hudson Ltd., 1970); figs. 2, 4, 8, 12, 19, and 21 from Harry Torczyner, *Magritte: The True Art of His Painting* (New York: Harry N. Abrams, 1979); figs. 5, 7, 9, 10, 13, 15, 17, and 20 from Sarah Whitfield, *Magritte* (London: South Bank Centre, 1992); and fig. 11 from Richard Calvocoressi, *Magritte* (Oxford: Phaidon, 1979). All reproductions are by permission of Charly Herscovici and the Artists' Rights Society, © 1993 C. Herscovici/ARS, New York.

An abbreviated version of "The Elusive Heroine: An Interarts Essay" appeared as "*La Belle Captive*: Magritte and Robbe-Grillet," *Comparatist* 11 (1987): 64–75, and is here reprinted, in modified form, by permission of the *Comparatist*.

Library of Congress Cataloging-in-Publication Data

Robbe-Grillet, Alain, 1922–
　　　[Belle captive. English]
　　　La belle captive : a novel / Alain Robbe-Grillet, René Magritte ; translated and with an essay by Ben Stoltzfus.
　　　　　p.　　cm.
　　　Includes bibliographical references.
　　　ISBN 0-520-05916-6 (alk. paper)
　　I. Magritte, René, 1898–1967.　II. Stoltzfus, Ben, 1927– .　III. Title.
　　PQ2635.O117B413　　　1995
　　843'.914—dc20　　　　　　　　　　　　　　94-17127
　　　　　　　　　　　　　　　　　　　　　　　　CIP

Printed in the United States of America
9　8　7　6　5　4　3　2　1

For Judith

Painting is mute poetry,
and poetry is a speaking picture.

SIMONIDES OF CEOS

Writing is the invisible description of thought,
while painting is its visible description.

RENÉ MAGRITTE

This **waking dream** *could simply be* **art**, *of which sleep,*
it is true, sometimes gives us fragments, but which
only a conscious effort allows us to reassemble.

ALAIN ROBBE-GRILLET

CONTENTS

PLATES   (as listed in the original French edition, with some dates and locations revised after Sylvester, Catalogue raisonné)

Two grants from the Camargo Foundation expedited the translation and the critical essay. Both projects were supported by ongoing grants from the University of California and the Center for Ideas and Society. I benefited from discussions with Camargo fellows as well as Russell Young and Michael Pretina, the foundation's directors. I also found helpful the discussions I had during winter 1991 with my colleagues John Fisher, Carlos Cortez, Mark Gottdiener, Diana Garber, Dwight Furrow, and Bernd Magnus at the Center for Ideas and Society, University of California, Riverside. The exchange of ideas on art and literature with my students in three graduate seminars was invaluable. I also gratefully acknowledge the assistance of Renée Hubert, Cynthia Skenazi, Judi Freeman, and Françoise Foster-Hahn in tracking down Magritte copyrights, Willis Barnstone's help in improving the translation, and Bruce Kawin's wise counsel in revising the critical essay.

I am grateful to Jeanne Sugiyama and to William J. McClung of the University of California Press for their heroic efforts in securing the copyright permissions and to Doris Kretschmer, Rose Vekony, and Dan Gunter for their invaluable help in guiding the manuscript into production and beyond. Judith's patience during eight years of copyright delays was exemplary, while Jan's, Celia's, and Andrew's willingness to whisk me off to Baja to "forget" the frustrations was always welcome.

I thank Clara Dean for her skill at the word processor and her dedication to correcting negligent spelling and typographical errors.

A special note of thanks goes to Alain Robbe-Grillet for his role in making the publication of this book possible.

In "The Elusive Heroine: An Interarts Essay," as well as elsewhere, all the translations from French into English are my own.

Alain Robbe-Grillet is one of France's leading New Novelists and avant-garde cinematographers. His works have redefined the novel and the cinema as genres, and his art has left an indelible imprint on the twentieth century. René Magritte, one of the world's leading surrealist painters, produced a body of works that have radically altered our perceptions of reality. This book brings these two artists together in the novel *La Belle Captive* and in an interarts essay, "The Elusive Heroine."

La Belle Captive is a translation of Robbe-Grillet's 1975 novel, which he illustrated with seventy-seven paintings by Magritte; "The Elusive Heroine," illustrated with twenty-one additional paintings, analyzes the "collaboration" between these two men. My essay examines the artistic correspondences between painting and writing within the novel and, more generally, between surrealism and metafiction. The title of the novel derives from six Magritte paintings also entitled *La Belle Captive* (*The Beautiful Captive*) painted over a span of approximately forty years. The two paintings reproduced here (plate 27 and fig. 1) date from 1947 and 1967.[1]

The French edition of *La Belle Captive* is a 157-page book in large format, one of

---

1. The 1967 version of *The Beautiful Captive*, from the former collection of Mme. Georgette Magritte, is reproduced in the novel; the 1947 version is reproduced in the essay. The plate numbers refer to the illustrations to the novel itself, which appear in the translation as they did in the original; the figures, which are discussed here and in my essay ("The Elusive Heroine"), are gathered following page 213.

Robbe-Grillet was not the first writer to have been inspired by Magritte. In 1964 Henri Michaux published *En rêvant à partir de peintures énigmatiques*. Tom Stoppard wrote a one-act comedy, *After Magritte*, which was performed at Theater Four in New York in April 1972. Paul Simon's album *Hearts and Bones* (1983) contains a song entitled "René and Georgette Magritte with Their Dog after the War."

eight collaborations to date between Robbe-Grillet and other artists in a variety of fields.[2] Robbe-Grillet selected and arranged Magritte's paintings within the text, part of which had already been written before he decided to illustrate it.[3] Of course, Magritte, who died in 1967, had no knowledge of Robbe-Grillet's project, but there is every reason to believe that he would have approved of it. Magritte's pictures do not correspond directly to Robbe-Grillet's written narrative. They are used instead as pulsive forces, as generative themes for an imaginary discourse that parallels the paintings, glosses over them, and contradicts them. Magritte's images and titles are pretexts for the novel, a text that simultaneously comments on Magritte's paintings while parading Robbe-Grillet's favorite themes. The mysterious, poetic, and ludic structures of Magritte's art encourage a form of literary production not only on the part of Robbe-Grillet, whose narrative voice is splintered and dispersed throughout the text, but also on the part of the audience, which produces meaning from the pictorial arrangements that illumine in oblique ways the cultural myths with which Robbe-Grillet is playing and the pleasure he derives from this creative parody.

2. The other painters with whom Robbe-Grillet has collaborated are Paul Delvaux, Robert Rauschenberg, and Jasper Johns. There are two photographers (David Hamilton and Irina Ionesco), one composer (Michel Fano), and one film director (Alain Resnais). The collaborations, in chronological order, are: (1) *L'Année dernière à Marienbad* (ciné-roman, 1961): screenplay by Robbe-Grillet; film by Alain Resnais (*Last Year at Marienbad*, trans. Richard Howard [New York: Grove, 1962]). (2) *Rêves de jeunes filles* (Paris: Laffont, 1971): text by Robbe-Grillet; photographs by David Hamilton (*Dreams of a Young Girl* [New York: Morrow, 1971]). (3) *Les Demoiselles d'Hamilton* (1972); text by Robbe-Grillet; photographs by David Hamilton (*Sisters*, trans. Martha Egan [New York: Morrow, 1973]). (4) *Construction d'un temple en ruines à la déesse Vanadé* (1975): text by Robbe-Grillet; etchings and engravings by Paul Delvaux. (5) *Temple aux miroirs* (1977): text by Robbe-Grillet; photographs by Irina Ionesco. (6) *Traces suspectes en surface* (1978): text by Robbe-Grillet; lithographs by Robert Rauschenberg. Only forty copies of the book were printed, each signed by both artists. (7) "La Cible," preface to the catalogue for the Jasper Johns exhibition held at the Beaubourg Museum in Paris, April 8–June 4, 1978. Instead of a conventional scholarly introduction, like the one Michael Crichton wrote for the catalogue of the Jasper Johns exhibition at the Whitney Museum, Robbe-Grillet's commentary on Johns's art is a piece of fiction that demonstrates the interrelationships of the two men's ideas and interests. "La Cible" ("The Target") was subsequently incorporated into Robbe-Grillet's 1978 novel *Souvenirs du triangle d'or* (130–50). Michel Fano composed the musical sound track for most of Robbe-Grillet's films, incorporating a dialectic between the acoustic and visual dimensions of each film. The generative relationships between sight and sound have their pictorial and textual counterpart in *La Belle Captive*. See Fano, "L'Ordre musical chez Alain Robbe-Grillet."

3. Part 1 of *La Belle Captive* was published as "Un Autel à double fond" in *Topologie d'une cité fantôme* (1975), 181–96. Parts 2, 3, and 4 were published in *Souvenirs du triangle d'or* (1978), 38–89. *Topologie d'une cité fantôme* and *Souvenirs du triangle d'or* were published without accompanying illustrations. The original title of part 2 (written prior to Robbe-Grillet's decision to illustrate) of *La Belle Captive* was *Propriétés secrètes du triangle*. The false student in *La Belle Captive* has a black notebook for a projected novel to be entitled *Propriétés secrètes du triangle*. These "notes" are reminiscent of Gide's *mise en abîme* effects in *Les Faux-monnayeurs*, that is, the novel within the novel and the different journals of the novel. For additional details on Robbe-Grillet's intertextuality and his other "collaborations," see the informative study by Bruce Morrissette, *Intertextual Assemblage in Robbe-Grillet*. See also David Leach, *Generative Literature and Generative Art*.

The shape of *La Belle Captive* defines her/it as an "open text" as well as a nouveau roman: achronology, contradiction, and proliferation of narrative voices create "indeterminacy," "discontinuity," and "dissemination." An "open work" such as *La Belle Captive* is, in Umberto Eco's terms, ultramodern because all the "openings" in the text have been placed there deliberately (16–17). The reader inserts himself or herself within the gaps of the story and the discontinuities among text and paintings, thereby producing meaning by organizing the disorder. The production of meaning necessarily involves the text and the audience. Marcel Duchamp once noted that the viewer makes the masterpiece; indeed, the image and the word of *La Belle Captive* need the collusion of the subject outside the text if meaning is to be produced inside it. The juxtaposition of pictures and text generates a new discourse—a presence within an absence—through which the audience derives meaning and strives for pleasure. This sensorial pleasure of eye and tongue and ear and mind transcends any simplistic synthesis of two art forms. It is a transcendence, the *Aufhebung* of an *Aufhebung*, a perpetual movement, a passing beyond that is capable of unifying separate discourses (image and text) by incorporating them into a new discursive genre: the *pictonovel*.

The 1967 version of Magritte's *Beautiful Captive* (plate 27) depicts an easel holding a painting.[4] The wooden easel is set against a curtain that obscures part of the seascape. Approximately one-sixth of the painting within the painting extends beyond the curtain, overlapping with the sky, the horizon, and the sea and duplicating exactly the portion of the sea and the sky that is behind it. This overlapping transparency of the canvas fashions a rectangular "hole" in the curtain, setting up a dialectic between foreground and background—a synchronic flatness that abolishes distance and space. The smaller painting is a false window calling attention to the signifying system of the larger painting. It is not, however, an abyssal device, a *mise en abîme*, for the hidden seascape, as the classical rendition of a picture/window would imply. It merely extends the seascape without a break and without miniaturization. Although the painting seems to be realistic, in reality it is not. Perspective is denied and flatness is enhanced.

Perspective in painting is a technique that serves the double purpose of suggesting, through an optical illusion, depth to a beholder who actually faces a flat surface and of clarifying, through variance in size, the relative position of figures and objects in a unified three-dimensional space. Perspective is a representational convention designed to enhance the illusion of reality, that is, the painting's mimetic qualities. In the late nineteenth century, the Nabis rejected an illusionistic perspective in favor of "a flat surface covered with colours assembled in a certain order," a rejection analogous to

---

4. *The beautiful captive* is one of the classical topoi of popular fiction. In the "Melesian" heroic novels of the seventeenth century—novels that evolved into the Gothic novel and later into the *roman noir* of the Fantômas period—a beautiful hostage, like the mermaid, was a mythical image verging on the cliché. See Morrissette, *Intertextual Assemblage*, 39.

Robbe-Grillet's later jettisoning of the conventions of fictional discourse.[5] A fictional realism that relied on plot and flesh-and-blood characters has now been replaced by a fragmented discourse in which the plot refuses to resolve along anticipated lines and in which characters with problematic identities proliferate. With the advent of cubism in art, perspective as a single point of view was destabilized even further. As in the nouveau roman, the perspectives of cubist painting multiplied into many simultaneous points of view. In Robbe-Grillet's fiction, characters move throughout the text engaging in a maddening complexity of contradictory events that emphasize the story of telling rather than the telling of a story. This subversion of plot, like the simultaneous points of view in cubism, nullifies mimesis and foregrounds the text.

In the twentieth century Piet Mondrian and Vasily Kandinsky painted pictures such as *Composition with Red, Yellow, and Blue* (1921) and *Composition VIII* (1923), paintings that refused to imitate nature. They did not describe or tell a story: they simply were. Although Magritte's paintings are not abstract, as are Mondrian's, Magritte's deliberate annihilation of space-time, when combined with internal pictorial details that contradict themselves, produces paintings (like Kandinsky's) that are objects. The upshot of all this is that Magritte's goal, like Robbe-Grillet's, is to create works of art that rival nature—a rivalry that opposes all a priori systems, including Renaissance perspective, well-established points of view, framing, and the logocentrism of classic realism.

Magritte's painting subverts its own system of representation by means of autonomous signs none of which is a real picture of the world. In *The Beautiful Captive* we see a big round object—perhaps a ball—on the sand and to the left of it another curtain, a curtain that seems to frame a stage set. These curtains, normally seen at the theater, dramatize not reality but the artistic process. They oppose the natural, emphasizing the artificial.

This opposition between the natural and the artificial results in a theatricalization of language, since painting, as Magritte points out in his *Écrits complets* (686; hereafter *EC*), is the visible description of thought. In literature, such dramatization foregrounds language in order to privilege the signifier over the signified, thereby calling attention to the signifying system.

Each abstract painting by Mondrian or Kandinsky, insofar as it is a flat surface using point and line and color, is an object that speaks primarily of its own existence. Magritte's art, unlike most representational art, demonstrates that painting can be representational *and* antinatural. Like Magritte's painting, Robbe-Grillet's writing— an *écriture* that draws so much from Gustave Flaubert, Raymond Roussel, and André

5. Maurice Denis (1870–1943) was the originator of the famous statement that defined the movement: "Remember that a picture—before being a horse, a nude, or some sort of anecdote—is essentially a flat surface covered with colors assembled in a certain order" (Hazan 79).

Gide, among others—is also simultaneously referential and reflexive.[6] *The Beautiful Captive* (both the novel and the paintings) is referential in the sense that it speaks of and portrays reality, albeit a subverted reality, while calling attention to its artistic design. Nothing could be more artificial, as Christo has demonstrated, than to clothe nature in red curtains, pink plastic, or giant umbrellas. In "Sur le choix des générateurs" (*Nouveau Roman: Hier aujourd'hui* 2:160 [hereafter *NRHA*]), Robbe-Grillet says:

> Today we have decided to fully assume the artificiality of our work: there is no natural order, either moral, political, or narrative; there are only human, man-made orders—orders that are necessarily provisional and arbitrary. And we laugh when such and such a critic scolds us for not writing naturally, as writers before us used to.

Robbe-Grillet wants his writings to be a permanent deconstruction of nature because he believes that nature, and by extension society (all societies, he says, claim to derive their legitimacy from nature or from God), always wants to have the last word. Robbe-Grillet sees his writing, which his critics maintain is antinatural and hence inferior, as an affirmation of the human against Nature (*NRHA* 2:172). He therefore stresses the artificiality of his own "constructions" while devaluing the artistic currency that is in circulation.

From Aristotle to the present, the fundamental aesthetic system has been based on the imitation of nature. Paintings are expected to be representational, fiction is supposed to imitate reality, and the title of a work must mirror its contents. To subvert this aesthetic, as Eugène Ionesco does in *La Cantatrice chauve*, is to destroy two mirrors. Ionesco's title has nothing to do with the play, even as the characters' dialogue, in its absurdity and implausibility, negates realism.

Magritte and Robbe-Grillet, like Ionesco, devalue realism and deny mimesis. The processes at work in their art are identical to nouveau roman aesthetics. For example, Claude Simon's discourse transforms the title of his novel *La Bataille de Pharsale* into "la bataille de la phrase"—a writerly event, not a historical occurrence. The title of Jean Ricardou's novel *La Prise de Constantinople* becomes *La Prose de Constantinople*; this second

6. In *Partial Magic: The Novel as a Self-Conscious Genre*, Alter defines the self-conscious novel as one "that systematically flaunts its own condition of artifice and that by so doing probes into the problematic relationship between real-seeming artifice and reality" (x–xi). Unlike Robbe-Grillet, who illustrated *La Belle Captive*, Flaubert refused to have *Madame Bovary* illustrated, arguing that the pictures would interfere with the novel's evocative power and the reader's imagination. Nevertheless, it is interesting to note that both *La Tentation de saint Antoine* and *La Légende de saint Julien l'Hospitalier* were "generated" by pictures: Brueghel's painting *The Temptation of Saint Anthony* and a stained-glass window of Saint Julien in the Rouen cathedral.

title, which appears on the back cover, shifts the emphasis from 1453, the date of "the fall of Constantinople," to the immediate twentieth-century problem of writing a certain kind of fiction. In each case, what might have been a readerly text has become a writerly event, and language no longer mirrors reality in any conventional sense of the word. Similarly, although Magritte's and Robbe-Grillet's titles evoke the image of a captive woman, her "representation," as in Magritte's paintings, is misleading. *The Beautiful Captive*, as a title, is essentially a metaphor enabling art to make a statement about itself.

The "beautiful captive" alluded to by the novel's title and Magritte's paintings is not a flesh-and-blood woman but a pictorial and writerly event. Thus, Magritte's *Beautiful Captive* dramatizes the artistic process as much as Robbe-Grillet's discourse subverts accepted realistic modes of writing; or, if you will, Robbe-Grillet's fiction dramatizes the writing process even as Magritte's discourse devalues reality. This change of status within the fictive body—a status that opposes the tenets of classic realism to the poetics of postmodernism—allows for bifurcations and metamorphoses that generate unusual narrative displacements.

The permutations of people, things, and titles within Magritte's art transgress the normal boundaries between the animal, mineral, and vegetable worlds in order to produce new "natural" laws: rocks that float like clouds (*The Battle of the Argonne* [fig. 2]), birds that grow like leaves (*The Natural Graces* [fig. 3]), bells that become flowers (*The Flowers of the Abyss* [fig. 4]), men who become stones (*The Song of the Violet* [plate 43]), and stone birds that fly (*The Idol* [plate 13]).

Robbe-Grillet also transgresses conventional modes on the narrative level by abolishing plot, character, and chronology. The voices and characters within the novel multiply and contradict each other, chronology reverses itself, plots self-destruct, the author interrogates the reader. A description of the inside of a prison cell abruptly becomes a description of the outside terrace of a café on the beach. As for Robbe-Grillet's women, like Magritte's, they are dismembered, "raped," transformed, and sometimes canned like fish. Nonetheless, for the most part these captives survive precisely because they are not real people: they are metaphors for the body of the text. This text is forced to submit to figurative mutilations in order to reveal the "secrets" or "mysteries" of language, cultural myths, and social codes.

In order to subvert reality, Magritte creates new objects and transforms familiar ones into something else, such as the baluster that becomes a tree trunk with limbs and leaves (*The Lost Jockey* [fig. 5]). He changes the substance of things or of people—for instance, the woman-statue in *The Flowers of Evil* (plate 5). He juxtaposes words and images, as in *The Interpretation of Dreams* (fig. 6), in which the word "bird" signifies "knife."

Perhaps because Magritte and Robbe-Grillet also violate the laws of gravity and of space-time, their uses of language, perception, and psychology relate their art not only to the thinking of Ferdinand de Saussure and Ludwig Wittgenstein but also to the theories of modern physics: Einstein's relativity, Heisenberg's uncertainty, and Bohr's complementarity. Their work, while dramatizing the arbitrariness of the signifier (Saussure), structures an inside-outside dialectic that stresses the ambiguity of perception (Wittgenstein)—an ambiguity that is also linked with the theories of relativity, probability, and chaos.[7]

La Belle Captive, like Robbe-Grillet's other novels, does not evolve chronologically; time is circular and the characters, when they exist at all, are not fleshed out. They assume mythic, bigger-than-life proportions, as in Magritte's *Portrait of a Woman* (plate 2 [1961]; a portrait of Stephie Langui, Emile Langui's wife); here Magritte depicts two men dwarfed by the enormous head of a woman. Magritte and Robbe-Grillet have destroyed the old Newtonian view of a stable and predictable world. They have done for art what the theory of relativity and the uncertainty principle have done for physics. They have changed our sense of time, space, and perception.

"The beautiful captive," whether painting, image, or text, lends herself to a variety of metamorphoses that further undermine the realism of the natural world. Magritte's and Robbe-Grillet's primary intention is to devalue the real in favor of imaginary constructions. They dramatize the artistic process at the expense of mimetic value. This reversal of the traditional role of art has led critics to assert that the reflexive artist has nothing to say. However, as Bruce Kawin states in *The Mind of the Novel*, the point of reflexive works is not that the artist has nothing to say, except that he or she is writing or painting, "but that reality and the imagination are mutually enriching and mutually sustaining categories" (212). Magritte's and Robbe-Grillet's art encourages a new artistic consciousness that allows for the commingling of the visible and the invisible, or, if you will, their art renders the invisible visible.

La Belle Captive dramatizes the mythology of art and woman even as Robbe-Grillet's text stages an imaginary dialogue with Magritte's pictures. If pictures activate the novel's diegesis, certain narrative passages provide answers to the mysteries Magritte leaves unsolved. In *Écrits complets* he says:

> [A door] could very well open on a landscape seen upside down, or the landscape could be painted on the door. Let us try something less arbitrary: next to the door let us make a hole in the wall which is also another door. This encounter will be perfected if we combine these two objects into one. The hole takes its position, therefore, quite naturally in

7. Suzi Gablik (96) states that although Magritte was knowledgeable in philosophy, he may not have read Wittgenstein. Nevertheless, as she points out, the resemblances in their thinking are striking: Wittgenstein was dictating *The Blue* and *Brown Books* to his Cambridge students even as Magritte was completing *The Human Condition* and *The Key to the Fields*, paintings that address the mental experience of "inside" and "outside"—the same mental phenomena with which Wittgenstein was dealing.

the door, and through this hole we can see the darkness. This final image may be enriched even further if we illuminate the invisible thing hidden by the darkness.

(EC 99)

Robbe-Grillet "enriches" the image by illuminating "the invisible thing hidden in the darkness." "Inside," says the narrator, "it is very dark" (below, 34). The word "dark" in Robbe-Grillet's text echoes the word "darkness" in Magritte's commentary. Having passed through the door we are now inside the theater, where the opera being performed is *The Idol*. Although Magritte's picture of "the idol" is a bird—a flying stone (plate 13)—Robbe-Grillet's idol, as it was for the surrealists, is a woman—the fair captive. Since we are dealing with "the body of the text"—both Victorious and Vanquished—we have yet another reference to the theatricalization of language climaxed by the burning shoe and the resurrection of the Phoenix. The flames from *The Ladder of Fire* (plate 14) illuminate the darkness and the stage even as the hot little key unlocks the mystery and provides *The Unexpected Answer* (plate 23), solving the mystery of the hole in the door. Although Magritte may see the darkness beyond the door as the mystery of death, Robbe-Grillet illuminates the stage of life.

Beyond the door each room or cell contains a "mystery" that can be solved only if the reader, like the artist, will play with the words and the "familiar objects" of the text. Magritte's *Dark Suspicion* (plate 12) unwittingly becomes a portrait of Robbe-Grillet (a man wearing a suit with a pen in his upper vest pocket). The man is looking at the palm of his hand, at the five fingers with which he writes, at the fingers that will turn the hot little key, unlock the mystery, and open the door. The hand turns the key to activate the dialectic between the inside and the outside, between the implied author and the implied reader. A hand, Magritte's hand, "draws" the curtains for *La Belle Captive*, even as he "attempts the impossible" by painting a woman into life. In *Attempting the Impossible* (fig. 7) a naked model is being painted by an artist. She is life-size, and they face each other, standing, as the artist paints in her left arm—the only unfinished portion of her anatomy.

Magritte and Robbe-Grillet have made woman their captive, yet they are in turn captivated by her. Their open-ended works require the collaboration of the reader or viewer. The task of the audience, as Kawin notes, is particularly complex because reflexive art presents itself as an artificial arrangement of falsehoods that are to be recognized as false (14). However, this endeavor generates the paradoxical truth that this seemingly "false" art represents the "true" underlying reality of the world. To unlock the door of understanding, the audience must set in motion the metaphoric and sometimes humorous slippage between word, image, and text. Without collusion and complicity there can be little insight. If the key does not fit, the door remains locked and the text remains opaque, obscure, and uninteresting. However, as soon as the key turns in the lock and the door opens, it begins to "play" on its hinges. The playing door is yet another metaphor for artistic license, for the artist dismembering or assembling reality. Says Robbe-Grillet, in *Robbe-Grillet: Analyse, théorie*: "Within the mechanism of ideology, the text is an entity that at any moment can play: like a door playing" (quoted in Ricardou 1:60).

In conclusion, burning objects record the pleasure of primary sexuality and the transmutation of matter. *The Ladder of Fire*, plate 15, in addition to the "hot key" (*The Devil's Smile* [plate 11]), depicts a burning egg and a ball of paper. *The Ladder of Fire*, plate 14, depicts burning paper, a chair, and a tuba, objects that Robbe-Grillet also incorporates into his novel. The role of the burning key is as privileged as the generative stone (*The Castle of the Pyrenees* [plate 1]), the egg, the cell, or, for that matter, the woman's shoe that calls forth the sacred fire. Paper and wood burn, but metal does not. Fire, however, gives them a common denominator. The pleasure of artistic combustion (*Le Jeu avec le feu* [*Playing with Fire*] is the title of one of Robbe-Grillet's films), like *Hegel's Holiday* (plate 34), combines antinomies and resolves contradictions.

Fire connotes life, pleasure, insight, eroticism, and art. Magritte and Robbe-Grillet stage these different facets of the creative process with play as one of the controlling metaphors. Nature is transgressed, art is dramatized, and language is theatricalized. Both men "draw" curtains and "open" doors so that *langue* and *parole*, the stars of the show, may perform their respective roles.

This present book attempts to draw the curtains on *La Belle Captive*: on the imbricated art of Robbe-Grillet and Magritte. To that end I offer first a translation of the novel and then a critical essay on it. The methodology that I propose for assembling this piece of metafiction, despite the gaps and contradictions between the text and the illustrations, will, I believe, give a coherent thematic reading of *La Belle Captive*. I have added twenty-one reproductions of Magritte's paintings that were not in Robbe-Grillet's novel because they also "speak" a text that is in search of the elusive heroine.

ALAIN ROBBE-GRILLET

RENÉ MAGRITTE

LA BELLE CAPTIVE

a novel

1

It begins with a stone falling, in the silence, vertically, immobile. It is falling from a great height, a meteor, a massive, compact, oblong block of rock, like a giant egg with a pocked, uneven surface.

On the smooth, flat surface of the sea, just below, the successive, motionless fringes of foam form a series of horizontal streaks that run parallel to the rectilinear shore of the beach. It is hard to tell, because of its no doubt considerable altitude, if the stone will fall on the blonde sand, or if it will split the sheet of water, where, once engulfed, after the spray caused by the impact has risen and fallen, it will leave no more than an indefinite series of concentric circles, suspended once again in a total and provisional fixity.

Fresh flesh-colored rose, suspended head-down in the embrasure of the wide, open window . . . Suddenly, ripping the silence apart, the cry of a woman is heard, very near, as though it were coming from the room next door through a partition that is doubtless very thin; the voice is young and clear, with a pure, warm, musical tone, despite the violence of the cry (as though a girl were being stabbed), which fades in a brief decrescendo. A vivid flower, the color of freshly wounded flesh . . .

[2] *Portrait of a Woman*

Or it might not be through the partition wall but through another wide, open window, also with a view of the white and blue sea. In the adjoining room, similar in every respect to this one (the heavy rectangular building could be an isolated beach hotel built toward the end of the last century at the top of a moving dune whose gray lines extend as far as the eye can see, in both directions; a dangerous site that would explain the disquieting state of its foundations and its cracked façade), similar to this room, as are all the other rooms whose identical doors, because of the effect of perspective, are aligned at regular, although progressively shortened intervals, on the left side of the long, vertiginous corridor that, on every floor, extends from one end of the hotel to the other, from the great wooden staircase that used to be varnished to the narrow aperture (almost a loophole) piercing the opposite gable at that distant spot, similar—I say—except, perhaps, that the fissures of the walls, branching out into a complex network on the surface of the plaster where the faded wallpaper is torn away at a number of places, become, here and there, veritable crevices into which one could easily insert the blade of a knife . . .

As I was saying: in the adjoining room, exactly opposite the gaping embrasure that would be cut in half if one were to extend the axis of the body laid out there, the murdered mannequin is now lying on the long, wooden, white-enameled table— described already—which, with a matching chair, constitutes all the furniture of this bare room. Let us also remember, in passing, the oval frame (without a picture) hanging on the wall to the right, and the receding perspective of the lines of the hardwood floor, lines that seem to extend beyond the window to where the vertical bars of the railing are silhouetted in black against the sparkling blue of the sea.

On the floor, in the foreground, stands an ancient phonograph with a large speaker that must be almost as old as the sewing machine mentioned above, which, because of its horizontal cone, has a vague formal resemblance to it. The stabbed body of the mannequin was found on the beach at the fringes of the dying wavelets, stripped of her clothes, her limbs bound and quartered by chains to the bars of a makeshift bed of fortune (of misfortune): the iron skeleton half buried in the sand, corroded and rusty, probably from a very ancient shipwreck, and, in any case, from what has been said, at least as old as the sewing machine and the phonograph.

In the immediate proximity of the latter (that is, toward the far end of the bedroom) and almost touching the blonde, half-tilted head of the girl lying on her back, her flowing hair hanging down to the ground like undulating seaweed, a man, scarcely any older (definitely under thirty), leans absentmindedly with one hand on the back of the chair of lacquered wood; dressed all in black—patent-leather shoes, formal double-breasted suit and black tie—and wearing gloves and a bowler hat, he seems to be daydreaming. He is tall in stature, and his features are regular and delicate. This

person may be the murderer, even though he is the spitting image, both facially and in terms of dress, of the two plainclothes policemen waiting for him behind the door, in the hallway.

All these are frozen in similar postures, their ears cocked in the same direction, listening to the cry of the victim recorded on the wax cylinder that reproduces perfectly every modulation. If the presumed criminal tilts his head a little more to one side, it is all the better to catch the last vibrations of the voice coming from the horn with the flared bell next to his feet. Since he has his back to the window, he has not yet seen the female figure that has just appeared in the opening behind the balcony. Smiling, dressed in a diaphanous beach dress of white tulle, fashionable in that era, and wearing a floppy translucent hat, it is she who is holding in her left hand, by the tip of its thorny stem, a red rose whose half-open corolla hangs its head down as far as her knee.

It is of course immediately apparent that the newcomer might be Lady H-G herself, and that the two adolescents in the bedroom are her children, the fraternal twins

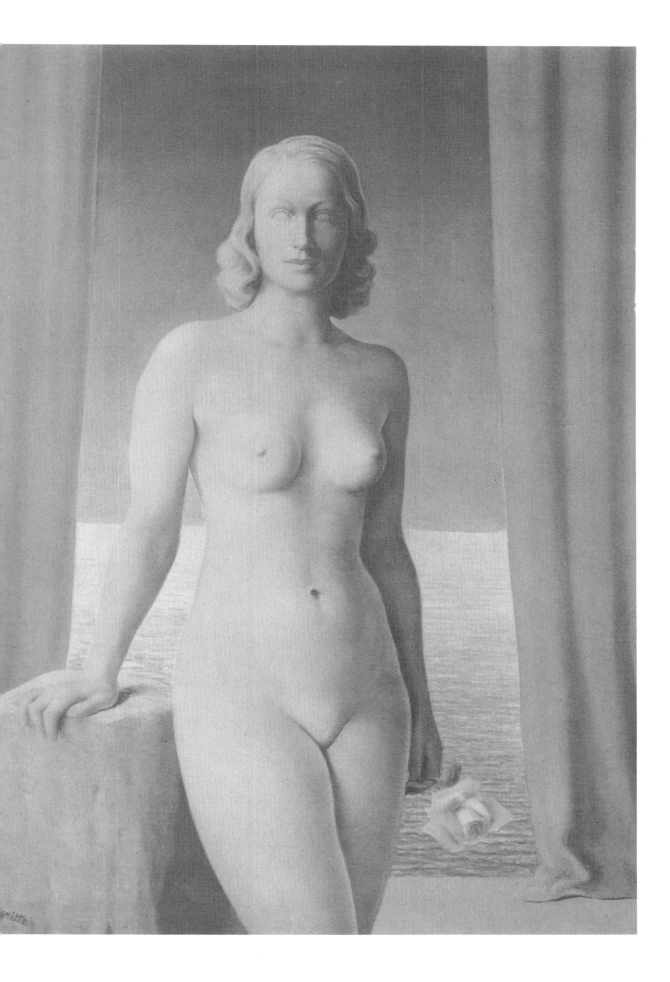

David and Vanessa: the girl still adorned with her light golden hair that exalts her large, pale blue, drowned eyes, and the boy, whose incestuous and fratricidal desires were manifest from his earliest childhood, as has been noted here and there on a number of occasions.

Nonetheless, there is a slight incongruity in the barely noticeable age difference between the precocious murderer and his young mother with the ancient, statuesque body. But let us put this detail aside for a moment in order, first, to list the principal and indisputable pieces of incriminating evidence. Two of these are visible in the hands of the policemen standing guard next to the closed door, one on the right and the other on the left, namely, the fishnet with the large square mesh in which the graceful body of Vanessa was imprisoned, like a surprised siren brought to the water's surface by a fisherman dredging for shellfish, and also the fat baluster adorned with multiple, bulging, more or less cruel rings with which she was deflowered. Each one of the other clues, gathered from the text and placed directly on the wide, converging floor boards, occupies one of the empty rooms that succeed one another the length of the hallway: the falling stone, the wine glass (apparently adulterated), the flesh-colored rose with the blushing heart, and so forth.

[7] *The Tomb of the Wrestlers*

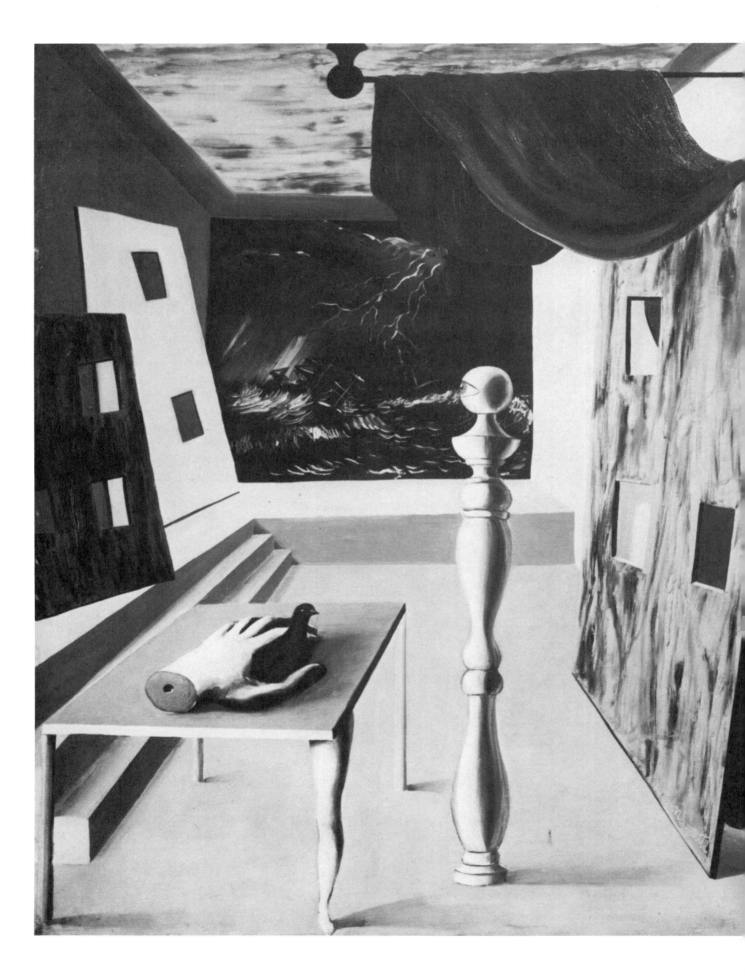

[9] *Memory*

A preliminary conclusion is in order: the episode known as "the difficult crossing" seems to contain a double allusion to the sinister vessel onto which the adolescent was dragged by her ravishers and to the outrage awaiting her there before she was thrown into the sea. Second (hypothetical) remark: the same, wooden, phallomorphic object could have served as a bludgeon for the young man's accomplices during the ensuing brief struggle, in the course of which David was apparently hurt; the small red wound on his temple next to the corner of his right eye must be the external mark that will, in due course, leave only a minor scar, whereas the murderer's total loss of memory would seem to indicate a longer-lasting inner trauma.

It would be idle to dwell on the story of the ship, an event already amply accounted for, or on the so-called rape (or on the metaphorical image of the bleeding flower); instead, and without delay, it seems to me very important to recall the reek of seaweed present throughout the hotel, whose musty, sweet, insinuating iodic exhalations are beginning to make me dizzy. I open the next door: this room is completely unoccupied, vacant, abandoned . . . But is not this the one that a moment ago contained the dark wine with the suspect color? There, behind the railing of the open window, are the busts of men wearing black suits, aligned in several compact rows, turning their identical, expressionless faces toward me: curiosity seekers, probably, attracted to the immense sandbanks by the sudden cry—assembled on a beach that, as already noted, was deserted only a moment before. I hastily close the door. In the next room there are, once again, the three white eggs, intact, nestling together in a small glass bowl that has been placed (by whom?) on the ledge of the gaping embrasure.

I realize immediately that this is a trap: if I pick up one of the eggs (for example, in order to examine more closely if there is not some telltale sign on the shell), I will break the closed circuit connecting the three tangential points, thus triggering the explosion designed to set the building on fire and destroy it completely. Then I hear footsteps in the hallway. I turn around. It is the doctor, who has already arrived for the official report. He is wearing his bowler hat and his long overcoat, carrying in one hand his small black bag marked with a golden caduceus, and with his other hand making

measured signs that seem to represent gestures of welcome, absent gestures, needless to say, whose excessive exuberance needs calming.

As for me, I greet him with a simple nod of the head as he passes. Then, on impulse, I cast a glance backward, only to note with surprise that he too has turned around, after several steps forward, all the better to examine me. In my embarrassment, and eager to regain my composure as quickly as possible, I grab the doorknob that is at hand—or almost at hand—in order to open another door, which is, this time, on the right wall of the long hallway. Is it the first available exit on this side? In any case, I don't remember having noticed any others before . . .

A new incident prevents me from focusing my attention on this problem: having suspended the projected opening with a mechanical gesture in order, once again, to look at the palm of my hand, as though the white porcelain doorknob had dirtied it, I register the real—very different—cause for this apparent change of mind: the door-knob has turned, but the door remains closed. I postpone the useless examination of my phalanxes. No time to inspect . . . I give the knob a shake. The door is locked (ah! ah!) without a doubt. I then notice the small, shiny key in the keyhole. Strangely enough, it is hot to the touch, although this does not interfere with the proper functioning of the lock, quite to the contrary, perhaps, aha!

[11] *The Devil's Smile*

[12] *The Dark Suspicion*

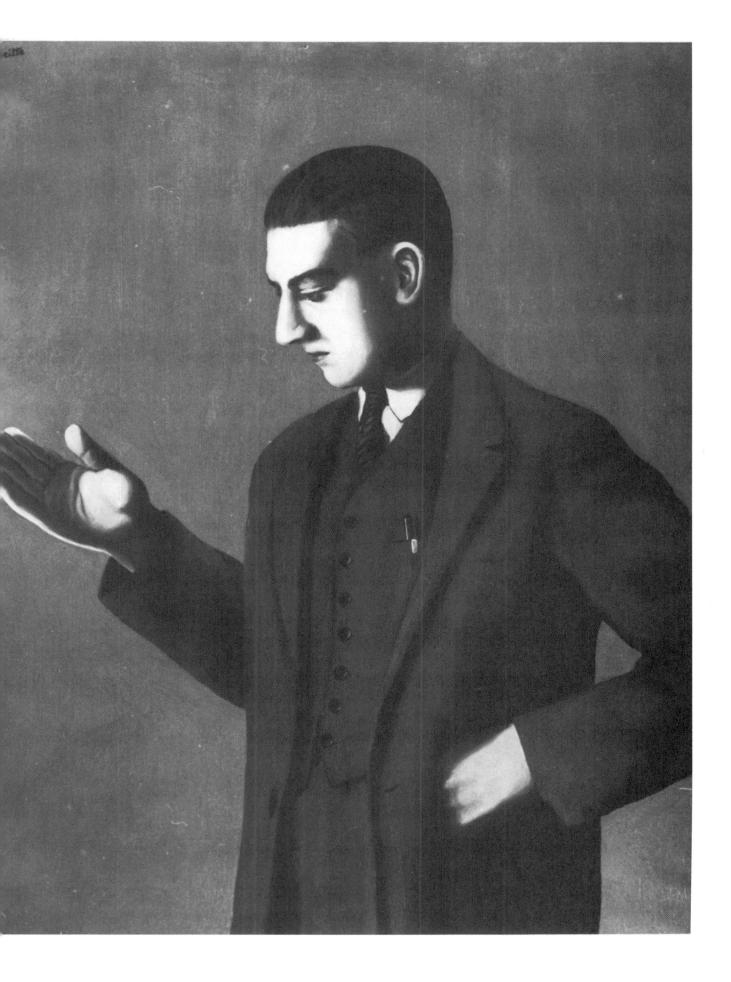

Inside, it is very dark. I enter on tiptoe. I arrive in time for the beginning of the performance. I take inordinate precautions not to disturb my neighbors and, without making a sound, I sit down on an unoccupied chair, covered in red velvet, at the back of the box. The heads of the spectators that turned around momentarily as I entered have now returned to their normal position, but, unfortunately, the black shapes sitting in front of me obstruct my view of the stage. I crane my neck the best I can and manage thus to distinguish an open-air hearth in front of which an adolescent couple is kneeling. Aha! I have seen enough to conclude that the name of the opera being performed this evening is *The Idol*, contrary to the announcement on the posters outside. Since I know the play by heart (and for good reason!), I settle down comfortably into my seat in order to reflect in peace.

A little later, after my eyes have adjusted to the darkness, I notice next to me a frail, young, blonde girl who is shifting to the right and to the left on her velvet chair in a vain effort to see the spectacle. Using the pretext of the word "pardon," which I had already addressed to her when I touched her by accident as I entered the box, I decide to help her by whispering into her ear a brief résumé of the plot, which—I say— recounts a little-known version of the legend of the Phoenix: in exploding, the egg gave birth to a big black bird whose winged form emerges from the flames. It flies over the sea for a long time, and then over the cliffs.

Scanning the earth with its piercing eye, it finds what it is looking for: a high-heeled woman's shoe lying in the rocks, the only relic washed up by the waves after the drowning of the female swimmer (already referred to) and the swallowing up of her sundry clothing. The moment the bird alights on it, the shoe ignites, of course, and immediately becomes an enormous pyre. Everything is consumed by degrees (which

explains, among other things, the abnormal temperature of the little key), even the brasses of the orchestra. Vanessa appears (wearing on this occasion, for who knows what reason, a wig as black as a raven's wing) since she too is in search of the lost and precious shoe. All that is left for her to do is to devour the bird. Since it has already had time to lay a new (parthenogenetic) egg, the permanence of the cycle is assured . . .

Suddenly my female listener seems to have been taken ill, as though my words—which she had been drinking in avidly—had poisoned her. Under the disapproving

[15] *The Ladder of Fire*

"shushes" of my neighbors, who have again turned around, I carry the now unconscious girl toward a small room of ambiguous uses, with which I am familiar and which
is not far away, on the other side of the hallway that leads to the boxes. I put her limp
body down full length on the rectangular table, which is covered with a thick red felt-
like material (can it be a gaming table?). But the complicated hairdo of the unknown
girl has come undone as I transported her, and her thick blonde hair is now hanging
down to the ground; this has the advantage of bringing us back to a situation already
accounted for (under the scarlet cloth, the wood is assuredly enameled in white).

The doctor in the long black coat makes his entry, most propitiously. Without saying a word, he opens his leather bag and arranges his instruments so that he can, without further delay, make an injection into the milky flesh of the beautiful and unconscious girl—flesh which, I would say, is now much less translucent than it had appeared in the semidarkness of the auditorium, illuminated only by the reddish and distant light coming from the sacred fire at the back of the stage.

In order to get rid of her scanty clothing and her elegant evening shoes, I throw them unceremoniously out of the wide-open window toward the darkness beyond

[17] *The Night Owl*

and the murmurings of the sea. A little later (how much later?) I am again walking in the mild, humid night, between the rows of tall façades whose state of disrepair has already been mentioned apropos of what I no longer remember; some of them are even in such ruin that it is difficult to imagine any normal domestic life taking place behind this succession of walls, with their disturbing cracks, condemned embrasures, gaping holes, and dislocated cornices from which, at any moment, a dangerous block of stone threatens to dislodge itself. I notice once again the shop—freshly washed, almost spruce, having survived as if by miracle in the midst of this gutted section of town—that sells communion and wedding dresses, whose sign "Divine Vanities" has so far lost only two of its letters.

Description of the shop window, the white tulle dresses, the mannequins, the changing room, the false bottom, its workings, and so forth. This entire passage is more or less familiar. A notable detail may perhaps remain: after leaving the Municipal Theater, in the middle of the performance, I crossed the big, empty, and dark square,

[18] *Pandora's Box*

where, under the yellow light of one of the rare streetlamps, there was a wooden table covered with some kind of cloth hanging down freely on all four sides; it must have been the stall of a fruit or drink vendor, since the reddish stain soiling one of the edges of the rectangle might have been spilled juice—pomegranate or watermelon—or perhaps wine. Next to it, a rustic stool, hewn from a tree trunk and mounted on four crude legs, looked like a chopping block.

When I next crossed the old bridge on the black river with its still, taut surface marbled here and there with gleaming eddies whose flow has been accelerated by the rising waters that have now reached as high as the vaults of the arches, a child of about twelve, a girl vendor wandering the deserted evening streets in search of an improbable, late stroller, approached, offering me the last rose in her flat hawker's basket. I paid the low price she was asking, but I did not want to take the flower, feeling suddenly a violent repulsion at the very thought of touching it. Having reached the far side of the bridge, I heard a muffled sound behind me, like a big stone falling into the river from a great height . . .

There also remains the problem of the empty picture frame, which must have a direct link with the little key, a hidden rapport that would undoubtedly require a long explanation. But I will have to quicken my step, having wasted enough of the limited time at my disposal while descending hesitantly the slippery stairs to the water's edge in order to wash my hands in the current as best I can amid the deceptive shadows that move ceaselessly at the heart of darkness. I immediately come upon this uncertain, desolate spot, an expanse of demolition yards, wastelands, high fences that sometimes hide the base of enormous, thin, temporary metallic structures, abandoned constructions, wooden shacks, and, farther on, this giant excavation, at the bottom of which prowl machines—rendered ridiculous by the distance—that seem to want to discover,

by the glare of their headlights, the remains of a civilization buried at unprecedented depths . . . Without stopping I also walk along the avenue lined with chestnut trees, next to the prison that has already been described.

Here I am for the moment, alone in the early gray dawn, before daylight, in front of my own open window that is waiting for me at the center of its façade, which, for the most part, has been condemned. A big mirror that occupies all of the visible wall behind the table (always the same one) reflects the bluish image of the house opposite, as though the outside of the room were on the inside, a deployment that is reminiscent of the fanatical temple whose outline I painfully retrace, day after day, through the retelling, the contradictions, and the gaps.

2

In the very beginning there is some kind of tumult, a chaotic movement of inter-mingled bodies, men in dark clothes advancing, jostling each other, or perhaps shoving someone in order to sweep him along with them down an indistinct, pale, fairly wide hallway, or even several hallways with no particular characteristics that would allow one to distinguish between them; their dimensions become progressively narrower with each succession of right angles, the result of sudden, irregular, and unforeseen changes in direction that occur for no apparent reason.

The stamping, the blurred gestures of arms and legs blending into a formless, mo-bile mass that presses forward in rapid disorder, the rustling of the black uniforms, the heavy breathing, everything abruptly disappears—and once more nothing remains but the empty, almost abstract hallway, as though it too were about to fade away, its white paint lacking quality or luster—but everything reappears suddenly in a perpen-dicular hallway that is in all likelihood even narrower, and through which the whirling cohort has difficulty in passing. How many are there? The tussling and the animated

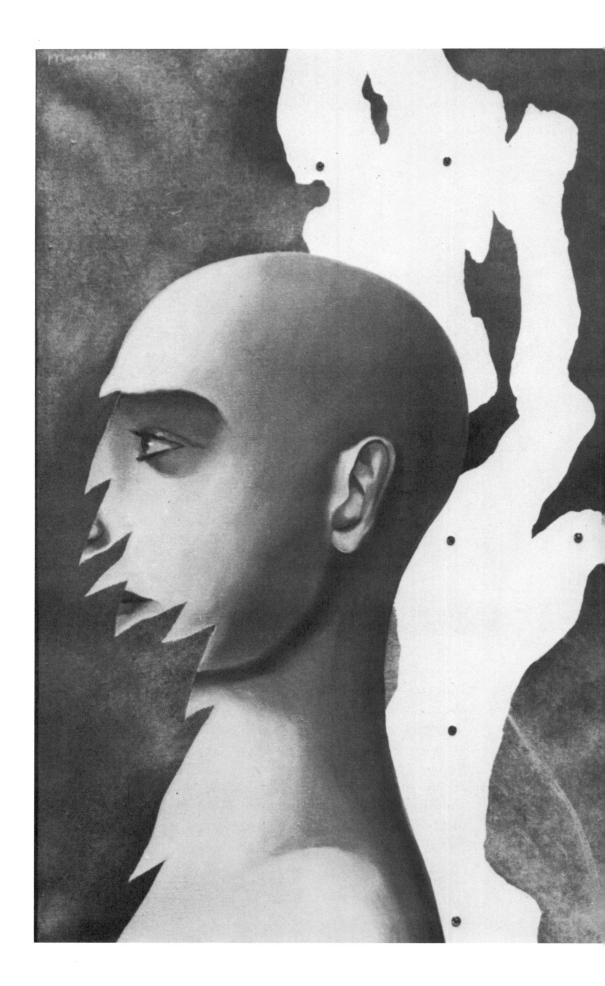

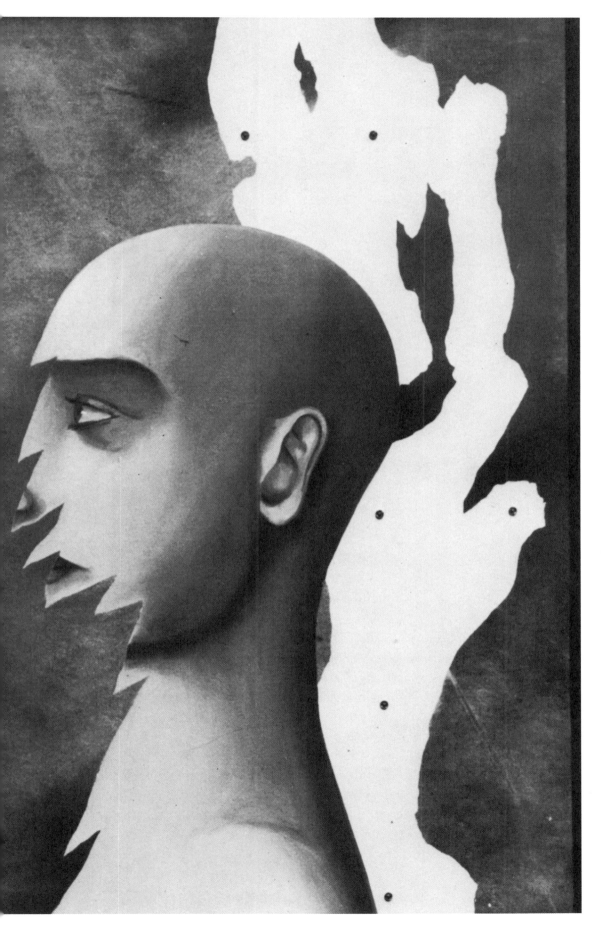

gesticulations prevent any approximate count: five or six perhaps, fifteen, maybe more, or far fewer.

The hallway here is so narrow that the heavy boots mark time; the mass of black jackets coalesces, forming an elongated plug that scrapes the blind walls with a multitude of gilded buttons, epaulette tabs, and wide leather belts from which bulge symmetrically the cartridge pouch and the holster for the heavy service pistol. But once through the bend, everything flows as though by enchantment, and the space momentarily disturbed is again white and empty. Then, a little farther on, there is once more the tumult of military uniforms rushing along in disorder, then again the empty hallway, and again the violent and chaotic troop, the empty hallway, the unfurling troop, the empty hallway, and so forth.

Finally the mass bumps up against something and a door opens, giving way under the pressure of the first forward elements. The black boots laced up above the calf have, in the space of a few seconds, step by step, come to a halt; the jodhpurs are in

turn immobilized. One last movement continues to agitate the formation above the patent-leather belts, chests buttoned up tight within each erect jacket with its little stand-up collar, the arms with one oblique braided stripe, hands in black leather gloves that seem to pursue with force a foreign body situated in the middle of the cortège, creating on the surface—at the level of the flat military hats with their rigid contours—a disturbance whose center moves forward by irregular loops, finally and suddenly expelling the intruder, like a pip being spat out, or like a cork being ejected by high pressure. The person thrust out is a man like the others, but different, wearing white pajamas, and the door closes behind him with a dull thud. Once more the dangerous agitation has stopped completely; but for how long?

Nonetheless, nothing more happens. The soldiers, whatever their number, with their empty faces and loose-fitting garments without markings or distinctive form, have vanished altogether. Who said they were even soldiers?

The man is alone, in the silence, in the middle of the cell. Little by little, and with caution, I realize that it is me, probably. The only other things of note are the two small windows, too high and secured with heavy bars, a wooden chair painted white, a broken mirror, nothing else. On reflection, the presence of the mirror is unusual in this kind of place. I approach the wall and lean toward the clouded, greenish, roughly trapezoidal surface: bounded on top by two right angles with ground edges and by a slightly curved oblique line with a sharp edge forming the bottom. I have difficulty recognizing myself in the framed image. They must have shaved my head several days ago, by the looks of things, since a uniformly black shadow covers my cranium, cheeks, and chin.

Slowly I rub with the tips of three fingers the main features of the proffered face: the chin, the right half of the mouth (the lower lip, from the center to the corner, then the upper lip in the other direction), the inside rim of the right nostril, the wing and bridge of the nose, the arch of the eyebrow. These are no doubt my features. But my entire physiognomy seems to have lost all character, all identity; it is a standard head, an anonymous form; henceforth I resemble the robot-portrait of the murderer that appeared in the newspapers and that, not very long ago, I found so amusing, whereas, cleanly shaved, my hair combed, dressed in gray, with that discreet and reassuring elegance that I have always been proud of, having left my car in a "temporary parking zone" available during periods of light traffic, and after crossing the promenade with

the stiff springy gait of the seriously disabled, a gait that I now execute to perfection by leaning on a special cane with an ivory-tipped handle, and then having deliberately chosen an isolated table, exposed nonetheless to the morning sun on the nearly deserted terrace of one of the many establishments that line the seashore, and having been met by a black waiter dressed immaculately in white who approaches in order to ease this rich and crippled client into the chair he has selected, and having ordered a large café-crème and two brioches, I settle down comfortably into my rattan armchair, my left leg extended slightly to one side, preparing to read from beginning to end, with the meticulous care that I lavish on such matters, as well as on many others, the article that has appeared in the latest edition of the *Globe*, that of nine o'clock.

Immediately I notice the first anomaly: the face sketched in black lines on a gray background is distinctly asymmetrical, whereas this not unimportant detail appears neither in the accompanying general description nor in any of the statements taken from the witnesses. While reading the text, I note also that the position of the body is inexact, as well as its location in the enormous assembly room of the abandoned factory. It is difficult at the moment to draw any definitive conclusions, because, in order to explain these modifications, at least three solutions seem possible (even though, to be honest, not one of them is altogether convincing): a journalist's error in reporting the story, the moving of the corpse by someone else after the heinous crime, a deliberate lie put forward by the police in order to mislead, or lull, or worry the criminal or criminals.

Nonetheless, I experience a mild feeling of excitement while reading about a particular detail of the staging, falsely attributed to the murderer, that suggests an interesting and imaginative mind belonging to whoever came afterwards, or to the writer of the article, or to a crafty policeman. I immediately sense a trap . . . Wishing, once again, to take stock of the possibility of an eventual return to the scene, I raise my eyes toward the bright line of the horizon that delimits the upper part of a flat blue sea whose lower border is fringed by many small, sparkling wavelets; the beach is almost empty at this time of day, whereas toward noon, it is suddenly swarming with people, a privileged hunting area where all I have to do is stretch out on the sand—with, at the moment, no infirmity or cane—in order to choose and operate freely

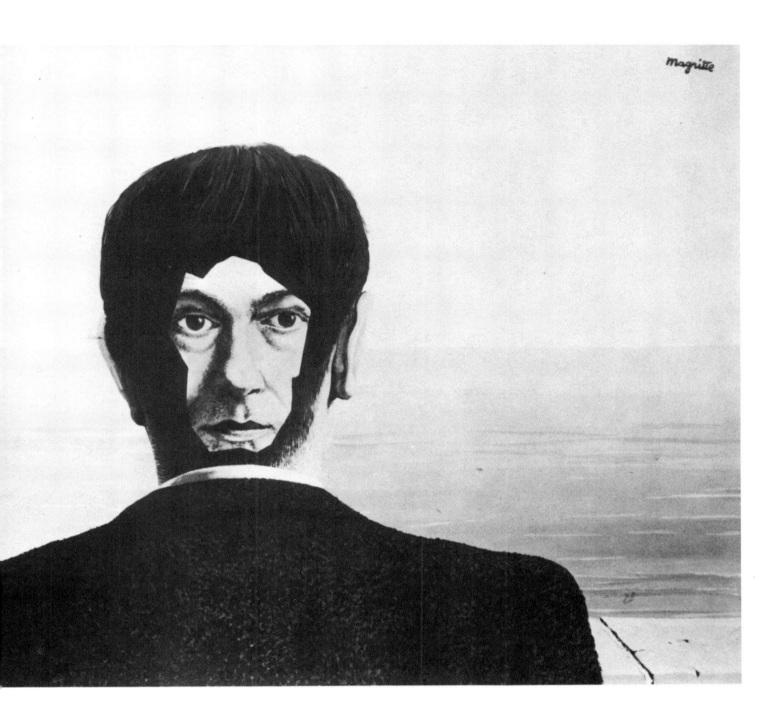

amidst the constant stream of golden, more than half-naked female bathers: this one, for example, a beautiful animal with blonde hair, rare for our climes, who today is playing ball with two other girls, seemingly unbothered by the crowd, whose unexpected interventions in the game elicit, on the contrary, incessant cries of joy; for several weeks now I have been observing and registering, episodically, the lithe contortions of her body, the dazzling flight of her hair, and her deep, throaty laughter.

At that very moment, as my gaze returns to the open page held stiffly in front of me with two hands, I discover a customer all alone—a student by all appearances—who has taken a seat, without my noticing her, not far from my own table, apparently while I was absorbed in my meticulous examination of the newspaper. She has placed a book and a notebook, both of them closed and covered with black paper, on the white tablecloth held in place by four metallic clips, a precaution against sudden gusts of wind. At this point I barely avoid a bifurcation toward the brief miniature whirlwind that buffets the crowded beach, and I resume by noting that in front of the young student, placed to one side near the edge of the round table, there are also a glass and a bottle (opened but still full) of red lemonade—a nervous system stimulant that universities consume in great quantities during examination periods. How could this late arrival have been served already, when I was unaware of any activity by the staff on the terrace, and have not yet seen the black waiter return with my own order?

At this moment, as though sensing she was being observed, even though my seat is definitely behind hers, the girl turns her head slowly in my direction; the perfection, the assurance of her movement convince me instantly that she knows in advance where her gaze will stop; she stares at me briefly, then, without a flicker of an eye, she calmly executes the inverse rotation of her neck and shoulders in order to contemplate once again the almost artificial stillness of the sunlit sea directly in front of her. Full, well-defined lips, large limpid eyes, a very long neck, small ears, a smooth and warm complexion, a firm curvaceous body without plumpness, the whole corresponding quite well to the nomenclature of "pubescent adolescent." One would say

that in order to display the shape of her breasts, which—seen in profile—seem braless in their rounded contours, she performs an elaborate and unpredictable gesture with her two bare arms, which rise slowly above her full black hair with its russet highlights to form an amphora, joining her wrists for a second, then separating them again with a double rotation of her hands, typical of Oriental dancers; from there her elbows fold forward slowly and come to rest softly on the tablecloth, where her forearms remain extended on each side of the black notebook. In its affected intricacy this graceful movement, seemingly designed, moreover—since there is no one else around—for the benefit of the stranger with the graying temples who, since he has delicate hands and steel-rimmed glasses, looks like a surgeon, with a view to exciting his interest (message received aha!) through gratuitous play rather than by premeditation, this movement strikes me as a sign that will, no doubt, decide the fate of the performer. I must now see her standing and also examine the way she moves. It is my move. Meanwhile, once again, the girl turns toward me; and for a second time I feel as though I am the object of her petrifying scrutiny.

There is a square judas measuring twenty centimeters on each side, cut into the door of my cell. The guards can, from the outside, open the hatch in order to pass a bowl or other object through it to the prisoner, or they can manipulate up and down the movable, slanted slats that have been installed on the mobile frame: five thick iron slats pivoting against each other along their horizontal axes. Between the second and third slats, now inclined at a forty-five-degree angle (even though I have not seen the strips move, nor have I heard the slightest sound of steps in the hallway), are now framed in the semidarkness—and protected by the small metal hood—someone's two eyes, fixed, brilliant, inexpressive.

The surveillance here must be part of the general plan for the behavioral modification of the captives, in addition to the injections, the incomprehensible interrogations, and the scuffles in the hallways. The metal slats have just closed, slowly and noiselessly, with a steady movement, so that each one overlaps the other by approximately eight or ten millimeters. When not even the slightest interstice remains (the sharpest tip of

a knife could not slip into the tiniest crack), the spy-hole hatch opens completely, and through it passes the arm and hand of a man holding some kind of small register covered with black paper. Instead of wearing the sleeve and gilded buttons of a uniform, this arm is bare, fairly white, although muscular, and covered with hairs. After a moment's hesitation concerning the appropriate behavior for such unexpected circumstances, I take two steps toward the closed door and grab the black book. The arm withdraws immediately and the hatch closes, slamming shut this time with a sharp bang. Then, afterward, it is the slats of the louver, once again, slowly opening.

I recognize the book: outwardly, at least, it looks like the one the fake student had placed near her on the small, round table of the café terrace and on whose cover five

delicate fingers with pink nails play nonchalantly, while she is still looking over her shoulder in my direction with her critical, searching, interested, and, in any case, attentive examination, probably. Even though I have no difficulty in sustaining her gaze (which is not to say that I do it without impatience), the girl is slow to turn her head away, barely impressed, it would seem, by my practitioner's diagnosis, which contemplates her body quartered already on the shiny, steel operating table, where she is immobilized by thin straps of black leather.

I make my decision. Without taking my eyes off of her, I move my right hand, which is still wearing the black leather glove, toward my stiff, extended leg and my

shiny, steel cane. I say: "Excuse me. I get about with difficulty and I have forgotten my cigarettes in the car." I then point toward the glistening Cadillac parked by the esplanade. Not one muscle twitches on the student's glossy sex-magazine cover-girl face, not even the slightest smile deforms the rosy brown corners of her mouth, nor do her long, curving eyelashes flutter over the light green of her large eyes. The fake student casts her translucent gaze successively on my orthopedic cane, on the big black car, and finally again on me; avoiding the slightest useless gesture, I in turn reach into the right-hand pocket of my jacket and, with the deliberate movement that a butterfly hunter uses not to frighten a rare, bedecked, and downy Vanessa, by pouncing with his net too soon, I pull out a bunch of keys and hand them to the unknown girl, holding onto the smallest key, the one that opens the left front door, with my thumb and index finger. "Would you please be good enough to get them for me?"

She looks at me, evaluates my overbearingly paternal smile, weighs whatever might be hidden beneath the mask of an inoffensive gynecologist or psychosomatician, and examines the worrisome and reassuring car, trying to decide if it is humanly possible to refuse to perform such a small favor for an invalid . . . I say, once more: "In the glove compartment."

Having made no sign whatsoever of communication or intelligence, the girl stands up and comes over, takes my keys without saying a word, skirts around the tables and chairs toward the wide sidewalk, crosses it, heads straight for the car, leans over to insert the key, and so forth.

Excellent demeanor, a graceful and supple walk, perfect figure; special praise for her very long legs that reveal her bare thighs between the high, white boots and a light, bronzed, silk dress, whose lower hemline, in keeping with this year's fashion, is very short. Having performed the different movements with precision and without embellishment, aware nonetheless as she bends over, one knee on the seat, in order to reach the glove compartment, that she is exposing her apricot-colored panties, accented by a barely perceptible twisting of her hips, she soon returns and hands me the shiny keys and the small blue pack, already open, obviously.

"Thank you," I say. Automatically, and as though spontaneously, I slide a few cigarettes forward, offering her, with the same gesture, the possibility of taking one. She hesitates. Her fate is in the balance. She selects a cigarette with two fingers. I cast a quick glance to make sure that it is not the one marked with a tiny red spot on the filter tip, which I immediately, of course, choose for myself. And, with the golden lighter that I have taken from the left-hand pocket of my jacket with my other hand, while putting away the pack, I light the two cigarettes, one after the other. The girl nods and returns to her seat. Will I never hear the sound of her voice?

Only then do I become aware of my first mistake: as a general rule I should never limp in this kind of scene. But it is too late. The effect is very rapid, because the student inhales the smoke, holding it in her lungs for a long time before exhaling slowly. After the third puff, she passes a hand across her forehead as if her head were spinning, which should be just about right. Without wasting a moment (knowing the very brief duration of the narcotic effect), I stand up and with the help of my cane— which I cannot possibly forget at this moment—I approach my victim, who has slumped backward in her chair, a vague death-smile floating across her lips that have parted at last, her arms hanging limply on both sides. The cigarette has fallen to the ground. A few furtive glances around reassure me that no one is looking; I step on the burning end with the toe of my shoe and bend down—with perhaps a little too much suppleness—in order to pick up this bit of compromising evidence and stow it away in one of my pockets. As I straighten up, I notice the waiter returning with my café au lait, looking at me, already upon us. Instead of completing my movement, I seize, in passing, one of the student's hands, pretending to take her pulse, but this time ostentatiously leaning on my cane. "This girl is feeling ill," I say.

The waiter is bemoaning his fate in a low voice in a language that must be South American Portuguese. The girl, disturbed in her dream by the activity around her, manages to articulate the word "smoke." I wait to see, before intervening, if the other person has understood the meaning of the syllable, which could hardly have been audible, particularly for a foreigner.

"She said: 'smoke,'" the black man haltingly announces after ten seconds or so, eyeing me with vague, suspicious misgivings. I answer immediately and very firmly: "Yes. Exactly what I thought. They all take them these days at the University. But this one does not yet have the characteristic facies of the habitual user. It would be best to get her out of here as soon as possible." All the more so, since two gawkers are approaching already.

"She needs a doctor," says the waiter.

"Has something gone wrong?" asks the older newcomer. I will have to act firmly, without giving them any opportunity for personal initiative; otherwise all will be lost. "I am a doctor," I say, "and my car is over there. I will drop this young drug addict at

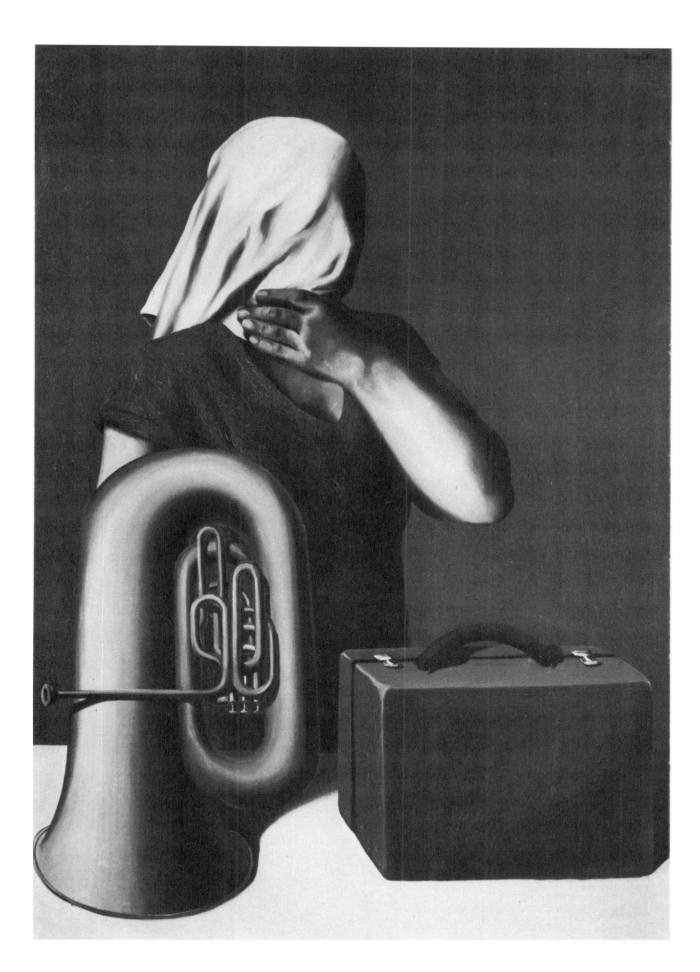

the hospital, since, in any case, I have to go there myself. Suppose the two of you carry her to the Caddy. It will not be the first time it has served as an ambulance!" If I may be allowed my metaphor! Aha! I add (strangely enough it is this last argument that persuades them to obey me): "I cannot help you because of my leg."

I myself have remained standing near the table on which the waiter has just placed the brioches and my café-crème (which is not, however, the one I had chosen), savoring the spectacle of the three kind delivery boys transporting my hot prey toward its black-lacquered coffin. It is the Brazilian in the white jacket who holds the girl under the armpits; the two idlers, apparently not as strong, have each grabbed one of her thighs; in lifting them higher than the rest of her body, the golden mini-dress has slipped across her stomach, revealing a pretty strip of satiny, light brown skin (it looks as though her whole body is uniformly tanned) above the tightly fitting panties that barely cover her pubis. Leaning on my steel cane, held firmly in my left hand, I unwittingly begin dunking a soft piece of my blonde brioche into the cup.

I must have swallowed several mouthfuls, judging from the level of the liquid, and eaten an entire brioche, because only one is left on the white tablecloth, when I become aware that the small group of people, whom I have already described, is waiting—how long have they been there?—next to the car whose keys I have neglected to give them, their three pairs of eyes staring at me. In haste I leave some change on the table near the second brioche, which is still intact, and head toward them, limping impeccably.

I ease myself behind the steering wheel. The others deposit the girl next to me, where she is now stretched out on the reclining seat, whose backrest I have just lowered by pushing the control button, thereby transforming it into a bed. This unusual arrangement, in addition to the red caduceus on the windshield, is enough to bestow their accreditation onto my borrowed profession. Moreover, the impressive size and serious color of the automobile give it an almost official air. Before starting the car, I take the time, under the solidified gaze of my porters, who are now immobilized less than two feet from the car, lined up as though for a parade, to write in the log, under today's heading, these few essential notes, which, from where they are standing, they cannot read: "9:30 A.M., Maximilian Café by the seashore, black Cadillac 432 AB 123, stiff left leg, ivory-tipped cane, medium gray suit, steel-rimmed

glasses, thin pepper-and-salt mustache." In order to verify this detail I run two fingertips over my left upper lip from the middle to the corner of my mouth.

All of a sudden, I have the impression that a crowd of gawkers is pressing against the tinted windows of the car, probably having run up from the beach in their bare feet, noiselessly, to join the first three witnesses who are still there, standing motionless in the front row of the crowd. With a single gesture I close the black book, which bangs like a pistol shot. In front of me, the louver slats are closed once more. Outside, however, there is the sound of footsteps and scuffling. The narrow hallway must suddenly have been blocked by one of the unforeseen changes in direction whenever the pack of dark uniforms and heavy boots is compressed into a tumultuous mass, whose confusion further slows down its flow. By cocking an ear, you can hear the

creaking of leather, muffled collisions against the walls, metallic clinkings, isolated exclamations that emerge here and there from a booming and as though contained noise that sounds like the sea; its intensity swells progressively in successive waves, until, after a few seconds, it becomes a deafening roar that ends abruptly and is replaced once more by silence. I listen intently, waiting for the succeeding, always sudden change, unannounced . . . But nothing more happens. Very carefully, I open the black book, somewhere in the middle.

A woman's handwriting, very fine and legible, covers the entire page with small characters in neat, regularly spaced rows bearing a title in the upper margin: Secret

Properties of the Triangle. If, in its six possible directions, you extend, infinitely, the three sides of any triangle, the result is a plane. In this infinite plane, the three tips of the triangle form a circle that contains the triangle in its entirety. Its three sides are tangential to a second common circle that is contained entirely within the triangle. The interior bisecting lines of the three angles intersect in the center of this second circle, while the mediators of the three sides—also allowing for a point in common—meet in the center of the first. When these two points are merged (concentric circles), the triangle becomes equilateral.

A figure, traced carefully with compass and ruler, illustrates this particular example. Contrary to the usual courses in elementary geometry, this triangle is here placed tip downward. Having once more verified the solitude and absolute tranquility of this section of town, already described—this muddy confusion of tumbledown depots and open fields where I have just stopped the big black car next to a billboard covered with multihued, shredded posters—and remaining seated so that, in case of emergency, I can drive away before the intruder has had time to notice my prisoner laid out beside me, working carefully and precisely with one hand only (the left one remains on the steering wheel) while leaning sideways over the languid, supine body, I slit the golden dress along its axis with one stroke of the scalpel, from the orange, silken triangle (stretched laterally toward the hips) whose upper hem reveals an incipient blonde fleece (also triangular, although of lesser dimensions and much more like the equilateral model), as far as the throat, where a small cross appears, held in place around her neck by a thin chain.

I then spread the two lips of this fringed slit that my blade has just opened, I fold back the two flaps of cloth on both sides, and at first glance I am able to confirm three of my previous hypotheses: the absence of any undergarment or lingerie, except for the panties already mentioned; the firmness of her young breasts, whose hemispheres are barely deformed, even in their flattened position; and finally the overall tan of her remarkably smooth, delicate skin, soft to the touch. As I have already indicated, if my memory is correct, the girl was placed head forward, the back of her neck resting on the edge of the seat, so that the loose curls of her abundant brown hair hang down to the floorboards.

I am immediately struck by the anomaly that this capillary coloring represents, dyed brunettes being much rarer than dyed blondes, particularly in this country. Two quick additional strokes of the scalpel, one on each side above the groin, confirm my suspicions by revealing the perfect triangle of her silken fleece, the color of pale straw, hidden beneath the superimposed triangular mask of silk or perhaps of satin, the color of ripe apricots. The exposed body, having thus lost its last protective covering, is now wearing only soft, high boots of white deerskin and the small golden cross. As I look at her half-tilted face, it seems to me I suddenly detect a slight movement of her green eyes, as if the beautiful sleeper were observing me surreptitiously through the long eyelashes of her half-closed eyelids.

This would be the time, in any case, to add the more lasting effect of a serious injection to the much too temporary one of the cigarette. Therefore, without dwelling any further on discordant pilosities, I grab the syringe, already prepared for the injection, from its case with the automatic latch. Since the position of the patient prevents easy access to the traditional areas, I decide to make the injection in the hard, amber-colored flesh next to the areola of the right breast; and, in order to ascertain if the girl is conscious or not, by causing her a very sharp pain in this particularly sensitive region, I insert the needle with calculated slowness, rotating it like a gimlet.

I seem to detect a slight trembling of her abdomen, a shudder followed by small, spasmodic contractions rippling under her epidermis, from the pit of her stomach to the pubis, quiverings that continue (and are even slightly accentuated) as the too-thick

[46] *The Agitated Reader*

liquid spurts into her flesh with a pressure that is much more brutal and rapid than necessary.

I observe carefully the sweet face of my victim. Her mouth seems to have opened further . . . And, once more, I have the impression that her dilated pupils are staring at me. Then, out of the blue, my second mistake, in all its magnitude, suddenly hits me: I have forgotten the student's book and notebook on the table next to the one where I stood eating a brioche. It will no doubt be very easy, under the circumstances, to identify the missing person and to begin looking for her. Also, a vague memory now crosses my mind of the café waiter in the white jacket on the other side of the closed window of the car, in the process of exchanging signs of complicity with his two so-called casual aides, as if in reality he knew them very well. As for my alleged prey, she may have perhaps held the smoke in her mouth a long time without inhaling it, with the intention of deceiving me, and she has, at this very moment, not without antici-pation, stoically endured this cruel injection, having earlier taken a powerful antidote.

At this exact instant, I notice in the left side-view mirror another black car parked at some distance behind mine in a clearly visible spot, where, not long ago, there was certainly nothing. There being no more time to undertake new sensitivity tests on my patient, in even more tender regions—whose results would, moreover, be very useful to me eventually for subsequent operations—I step on the accelerator, since the engine has been idling, only to notice immediately a change in the sound of the cylinders, which are normally much more quiet. I drive off, nonetheless, without even taking the time to withdraw the small syringe, which has remained planted vertically in the breast of my cumbersome passenger, so deeply did I sink the needle in it.

It is no longer feasible, under the circumstances, to make the anticipated delivery to the fake boutique, which I drive by without slowing down, and without even casting a glance at the smiling mannequins in the display windows that are dressed in white, diaphanous gowns. Leaving the ruined section of town behind me, I cross once again—

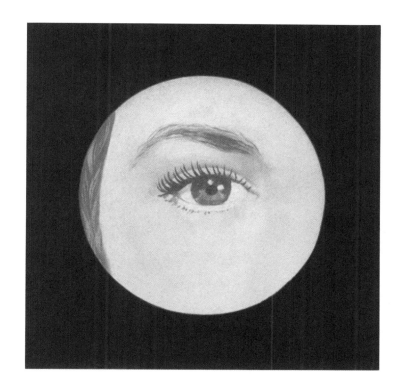

in the opposite direction—the bridge on the river swollen by the rising water. The little salesgirl, hoping to move me, extends her hand toward me, holding the one remaining rosebud; today, however, I can't imagine stopping to take it from her.

On the other side of the old bridge, in front of the Opera, is the spacious square planted with trees. The performance has no doubt ended, since a flood of spectators dressed in black suits and long dresses flows simultaneously through the three big doors at the top of the steps, as though they had rushed out with the sole intent of seeing me pass. Soon it is the boulevard along the sea, empty at this hour, on which I am driving at a brisk pace toward the abandoned factory. There I plan to rid myself of my false captive by throwing her into the water at the far end of the covered float, after tying her hands behind her back, just in case, to be sure that she will not be able to swim.

Is it the abnormal sound of the motor—which has become most worrisome—that makes me change my mind? The fact remains that as I pass by the ruins of the old deluxe hotel, the gaping embrasures of the ground-floor windows (easily reached from the terrace by straddling the railing of the small balconies) give me a new idea, which seems preferable, although I cannot clearly explain its advantage: I will lay my graceful burden down in one of the rooms, where at my leisure . . .

A sharp pinpoint of pain in the fleshy portion of my right arm, as I check the road in the rear-view mirror, makes me lose . . . Yes, it was indeed the sensation of an injection . . . The disturbing awareness of my third mistake crosses my mind (a second syringe hidden in the cuisse of one of the white deerskin boots) before I . . .

Then it begins again: the muffled footsteps in the hallway, the sound of the louver slamming, the silence and the long, deserted beach, the stone falling, and so forth.

3

Immediately afterwards, the interrogation resumes. The investigators are generally two in number, and it is difficult to distinguish one from the other. They stand side by side. They never change places. As far as I can tell, they always wear their long black buttoned-down coats and their bowler hats crammed down over their heads. When asking their questions, they speak alternately, but they communicate with each other only with wordless gestures, brief, slow, infrequent, and measured movements with one hand, and perhaps also with the head, although it is impossible to confirm this because of the very bright floodlights arranged in such a way as to blind me each time I try to look at their faces. One of them seems to be holding the curved handle of an umbrella cane, and he taps the ground with what must be its metal tip each time he wishes to interrupt me.

For the booby-trapped alleged student to have hidden a syringe against her thigh under the soft leather of a high boot, it would have been necessary for her, in effect, to have been wearing such a shoe. Yet in fact the white boots did not appear until very

[52] *The Presence of Mind*

late in your defense system: on the contrary, throughout the entire first half of your text, you spoke of a high-heeled shoe, which is very different. Do you remember this passage?

Of course! The detail is correct and I remember it very well; it seems to me like an easy answer, since earlier it referred to the drowned girl with the blonde hair floating like seaweed, whose big bird of prey—according to the legend alluded to—finds one of the shoes with the broken heel at the base of the cliff.

Are you quite sure that this story is about a bird and not about a big fish? Some kind of salmon, for example, that might have retrieved the sacred object from the sea in order to bring it back to shore?

No. If the word "salmon" was mentioned it can only be in order to evoke the flesh-colored rose that has been referred to several times. The only fish involved would be the girl herself, when the sailors brought her back to the surface, caught in their fishing nets.

Yet the factory by the sea, which you admit was the place you were going to, does happen to be a cannery, does it not?

I don't know . . . In any case, as I was careful to state at the outset, it is abandoned.

Let us come back to the topic of the tables, not the long, rectangular table on which you placed your victim in an empty room of the ruined hotel, but the . . . shall we say the cast-iron pedestal tables lined up on the terrace of the Maximilian Café. It is not clear from your narrative—burdened as it is with detailed information of minor importance—if the waiter in the white jacket placed your drink on the student's table or on the one at which you were sitting.

Neither of the above. He placed the cup of coffee and the small basket of brioches on a third table that was set back slightly, thereby forming with the other two a kind of isosceles triangle, or something like it . . . (Violent sound of the iron-tipped cane striking the ground repeatedly, tapping with a nervous rhythm.)

Is that why you neglected to take the black notebook with you?

What black notebook? I don't know what you are talking about.

That sort of memo pad in which the false student was writing her own account as she went along, whose contents are familiar to you, despite what you now affirm; even the sentence in which you indicate the arrangement of the tables proves it once again. However, you begin by asserting that the adolescent had not yet touched her drink (because the small bottle placed on the table—which could not have been brought by the waiter—was still full when you intervened), and you then suggest that she had taken an antidote because she anticipated your attempt to condition her by means of the intramuscular injection administered shortly thereafter. How could this alleged antipoison have worked if your patient had not even had the time to drink it? Let us proceed in an orderly fashion and go back to the beginning: what is the exact shape of the tables?

They are round—what I mean is: the top is circular—and the leg is in the center of a very heavy triangular (equilateral) mount. They have already been described in the report, along with the square tablecloths held in place by the four metallic clips, a precaution against the frequent gusts of wind that sweep up and down the beach.

Why do you never speak of the apple the girl was eating?

Yes, it's true, there is also an apple. It is one of the pieces of incriminating evidence, and each item is set inside one of the listening rooms that line the hallway from one end to the other. I don't know if the acoustic soundings inside have succeeded in revealing the suspected message or not. In any case it is not the student who was holding this big apple in one hand, which she would bite into from time to time with small white teeth, neatly spaced between her laughing lips: this last adjective in particular is hardly suited to her inscrutable demeanor. It would probably have been

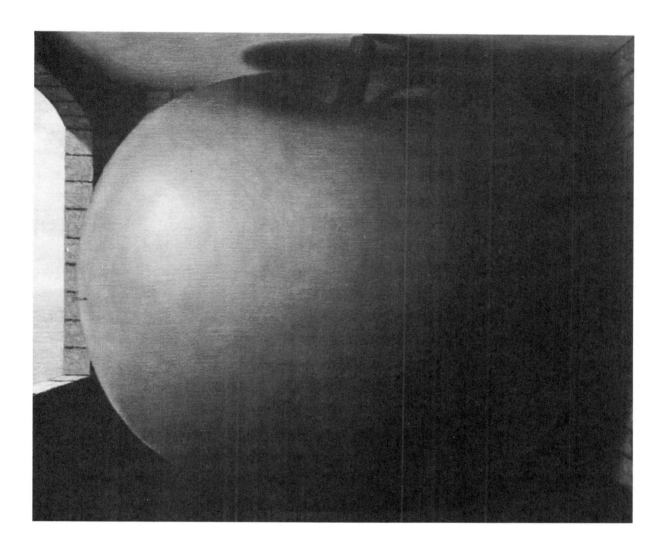

[56] *Black Magic*

the girl in the swimsuit, with the golden hair and golden body, who was playing ball with two girlfriends in the midst of the crowd, when a brief whirlwind suddenly buffeted the long beach from one end to the other, snatching up wrappers, newspapers, tablecloths, students' notebooks, and light clothing strewn on the sand by the swimmers, whirling them several meters into the air, even seizing tents and parasols here and there, dragging them with improbable debris toward the suddenly turbulent water. Packing cartons, strips of wood, pieces of children's games, wind-strewn leaves—all blend in the blue-and-white sky with the big seabirds that look as though they too had been torn apart by the wind . . .

This apparently unexpected, although dramatic, return of the phantom bird could provide a possible connection with an analogous storm that once accompanied the birth of the idol on the sacrificial ship. But I'm afraid of losing my narrative thread if the course of events concerning the apple with the message, whose predictable outcome should normally end up in this factory, which, before its closing, once produced cans of big fish preserved in hot sauce, if the events—as I was saying—concerning the apple are not taken up as quickly as possible: here I am sitting on the beach in my comfortable rattan chair, only a few meters from the water, which is dying in imperceptible, murmuring, and tranquil wavelets on the mild incline of wet sand where the continuous ebb and flow leaves changing festoons of white foam, like lines of bubbles in truncated arcs that vanish immediately. This movement of the waves, and the fragments of seaweed or shells that they roll with them today, this rocking back and forth, prompt me to return to two essential remarks concerning the idol—remarks that I'm afraid I will in due course forget, unless I note them in passing: among the objects dragged into the sea by the preceding gust of wind there was—coming from who knows what outdoor game—a piece of wood turned on the lathe, approximately thirty-five centimeters high, and a thin piece of plywood cut in the form of a woman's silhouette, approximately the size of a real girl; second point: the wind was so strong that it could very well have carried away more compact items, such as a woman's high-heeled shoe, which, in a few seconds, would also have disappeared out to sea.

Let me resume. Slumped in my rattan chair, I look somewhat like a fisherman casting, like someone waiting for a good bite, while holding in one hand firmly—not a supple rod inclined toward the horizon—but this thin cane of an invalid (described already) with whose tip I hit, with feigned distraction, some hard object . . . I no longer know what . . . formless, unidentifiable flotsam abandoned by the storm, whose force,

undoubtedly, would have been able to lift into the air the big, light, salmon-pink ball, which, without pausing for a moment, describes a mobile triangle in perpetual deformation, as it bounces between the graceful bodies of the three players (one particularly—as I said—is remarkable), and to carry it away into the sky where it would now be floating above our heads, an airship monitoring the shoreline, it too now captive, equipped with a basket as motionless as a vulture, observing with a spyglass the elusive prey that I myself covet, biding my time, and, despite her sudden, lively, unpredictable movements, not taking my eyes off her supple body, which bends to the right and to the left, then backward, suddenly, in a curving leap that arches her loins in accordance with the expected, alleged, or even simulated needs of the game in progress.

In the palm of her left hand, the young virgin is also holding an apple, gripped firmly between her thumb and little finger. She has not yet bitten into it, and it hardly seems to hinder her whenever she catches the ball with both hands, as though, on the contrary, her pleasure were enhanced by this exercise of skill, or at least in the public demonstration of it. It would obviously be very easy to entice her on some pretext or other into the boutique with the secret room at the back, by declaring, for example, that her skills have just won a beach prize, a prestigious victory for which she will receive a made-to-measure bridal gown, or to propose instead, with all sorts of

specious guarantees, that she pose as a model for photographs that are going to illustrate and launch a new fashion in a well-known magazine. In either case, the final scene is identical, as well as the decor: the dressing booth with the secret exit, where the altering of a pleat below the hip allows the ostensibly awkward operator to thrust a specially prepared dressmaker's pin into the top of the buttock, this time with a single movement; obviously it is a hollow needle that discharges beneath the tender skin the powerful narcotic contained in the small red bulb serving as the pinhead, which need only be squeezed hard between thumb and forefinger in order to discharge the venom. Immediately the victim falls into my arms, languidly, and all I have to do in order to alert those who will carry her to the other side, toward the cruel fate reserved for young goddesses, is to tap a coded rhythm with the tip of my cane— three sharp raps against the . . . (The interrogator interrupts me once again.)

You spoke, a few moments ago, of seaweed and a shell. What exactly are you alluding to?

The seaweed—according to what has been stated, even repeated on several occasions—is a metaphor designating the long blonde hair, with its warm tones and amber highlights, whose curls stir gently in the swell between the rocks, against the blue-green background of the deep water. As for the seashell, it can only be some kind of

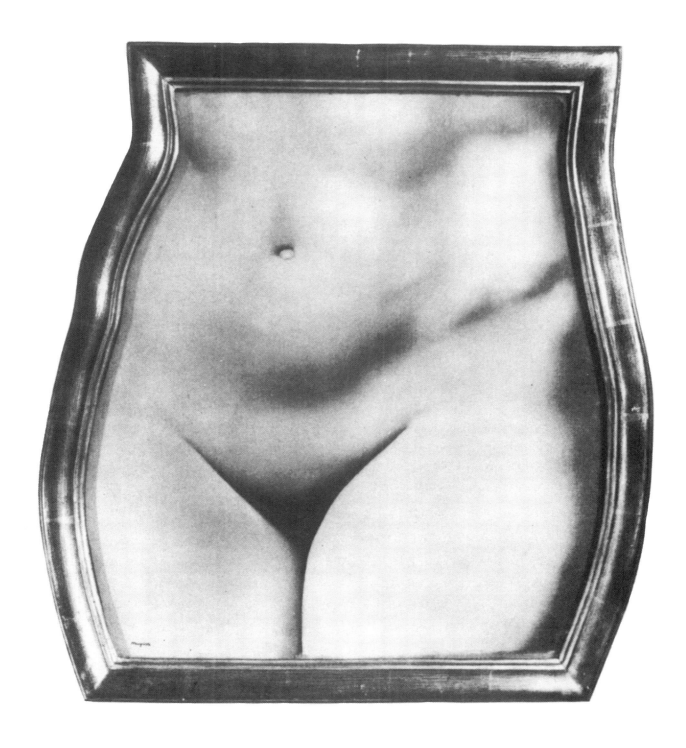

cowrie, whose inside is a vivid rose color, and the opening a narrow slit with crenated edges. It has an oval form, for the most part, with a convex upper part; occasionally, more or less elongated and sinuous rays flare out around the slit. Since the object is so familiar, it would serve no further purpose to describe it.

Is there a connection (and, if so, what is it) between this representation and the soap-sponge, the lemon, the small jug with the spout, and so forth?

An obvious connection! Of a sacrificial order, without the slightest possible doubt. The sponge soaked in acid is inserted into the opening of the shell . . . Surely you are familiar with the effect that lemon juice has when squeezed on the flesh of an oyster, and the way the delicate membraned fringes retract under the burning.

Was it this phenomenon that you were alluding to in your description of the evening at the Opera House, when you pronounced the words "glowing fire"?

To that phenomenon, if you wish, or to many other similar ones, that would all, more or less, be directly related to the consecration of an adolescent idol destined for future adorations. The sacrificial table has been on the inventory for a long time, as well as the phallic toy, the cigar of the false voyeur, the candle, the burning tampon, and so forth.

Is the virginity of the subject indispensable?

In theory, yes. But for selected novices, captured without prior examination, it often happens that earlier mistakes are ignored (provided the traces are not too visible),

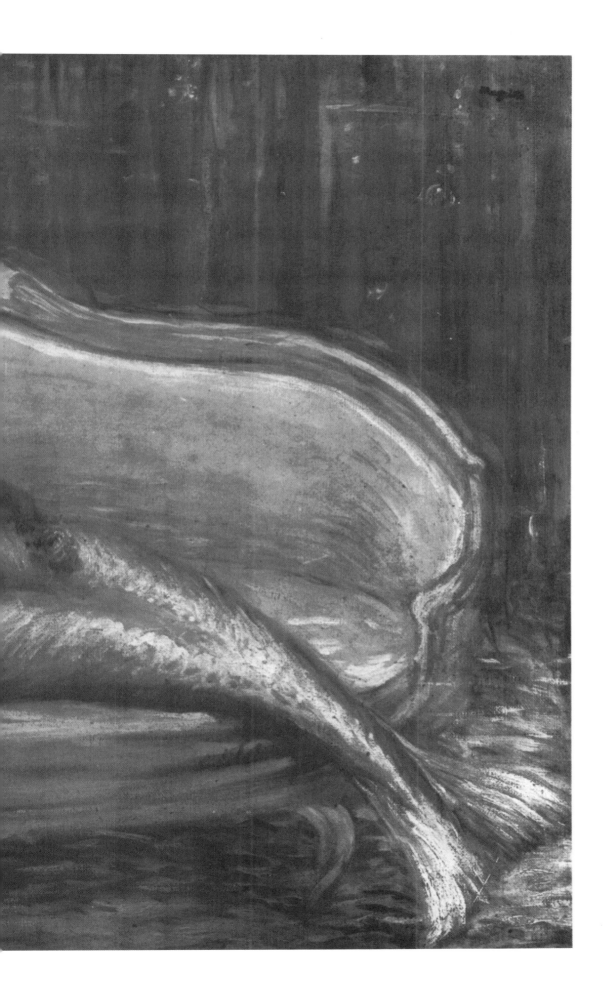

but they must nonetheless be atoned for by additional humiliations and cruelties in the course of special expiatory ceremonies. When, by contrast, a prisoner is discharged, for whatever reason, she is delivered to the cannery and marketed, after suitable cutting and preparation, under the label "Salmon and Spice." You will have no difficulty recognizing these cans by their pretty decorative mermaids whenever you see them piled up in the supermarkets. However, if the word "virgin" shocked you a little while ago, you may, if you wish, replace it with another term more to your liking: undine, infanta, fiancée, schoolgirl, and so forth. However, avoid the expression "doe-bodied maiden," which, if my memory serves me, has already been used elsewhere.

What happens to the chosen girls?

This subject has been treated in detail elsewhere in the text. Let me summarize: they become little minor goddesses, adored by the faithful in the temple of phantasms and lost memories whose elaborate architecture constitutes a kind of giant replica of the Opera House, a similarity that has often caused unscrupulous historians to confound the two buildings. In the entrance to the hallway, on either side of the wide dual spiral staircase, stand the two monumental statues of the ancient divinity of pleasure in her double appearance: Victorious Vanadis and Vanquished Vanadis. The performances are held every night, simultaneously, on the spacious central stage and in the

many private (or individual, or solitary, or anything you wish) chapels, whose imposing or secret doors succeed each other in identical series from one end to the other of the semicircular corridors, as well as the long straight hallways that crisscross the upper floors, not to mention the labyrinths occupying the various basements.

Why are the hallways always deserted, whereas the beach is sometimes "deserted" and at other times "crawling with people"?

I don't know. It seems to me, however, that the difference is not as pronounced as you say it is. There are occasionally lone strollers walking along the water's edge where the waves are breaking, bending down from time to time to pick up a shell in order to examine it, or smell it, or else gathering around a large piece of jetsam freshly washed ashore in order to contemplate it, and on whose fate they exchange interminable commentaries. Also, at certain times, crowds of people throng the hallways, marking time with their feet, whenever they are stopped by a right angle or a sudden narrowing . . . These men, who are perhaps soldiers, are wearing heavy hobnailed boots . . .

When you said that the twin Vanessa devours the firebird at the end of the show, what did you mean by that?

It is probably another sexual metaphor, like everything else. If this passage seems superfluous to you, you may eliminate it, even though it represents an interesting inversion of one of the preceding episodes: the one with the canned fish. You may even finish the report yourself, if you think you can do it better than I can.

Are you tired?

Yes, a little, inevitably: when, every day, you have to repeat the same old stories . . . lost . . . Still, I wanted to mention a few more ritual scenes that are enacted in the night palace; for example, the one whose title is "the beautiful captive," whose ankles are held in place by heavy chains and cast-iron balls, and also the rosy crucifixion with the sponge already mentioned . . . already mentioned . . . already mentioned . . . or perhaps also the picture of the bride stripped bare on a machine, which, in any case,

comes after the beginning referred to above: the photograph on the red-and-black prayer stool, hands bound with a rosary, the hat pins, and so forth. Old phantoms . . . Old phantoms . . . And always the interminable succession of doors, whose number seems to have increased since the last time . . . The most urgent course under the circumstances (fading memory, the uninterrupted tappings of the cane, the threatening weather, and so forth), the most efficacious solution, for the moment, would be to return to the violent odor of seaweed that reigns in these hallways. I have always wondered if it came from the greenish paint covering the walls or from something else: from the uniform jackets, for example, whose insistent presence again surrounds me, or perhaps from belts, cartridge pouches, and shoulder straps, or from the boots

themselves . . . Once more it is the chaotic rush, the tumult, the shocks inside my cranium, like a hammering whose rhythm is accelerating, whose intensity swells into an uproar.

And then, suddenly, nothing, except the faint, soft, crystalline, barely audible sound of isolated drops after a rain, flowing through the cracks of the gutted building, forming, here and there, small blackish puddles in which the rubber soles slip and slide with a squishing sound. Not far away a fire is burning in the darkness, and its crackling blends with the sputtering of the water on the sheet metal; it is one of those fires that demolition workers light in order to destroy unusable boxes, and to cook on the embers their meager meal of potatoes or fish.

4

Well, it must be morning once again, with the quivering of things in the white light of awakening. Sleep has been too brief, too agitated, interrupted by incessant breaks . . . I have a vague recollection of coming home late at night, or even at dawn, when the sky is already bright, when the windows nonetheless light up the silhouettes of the rare buildings that remain standing in this wasteland of work yards and ruins, their four or five disproportionate stories looming like scattered rocks against the seashore. Formerly opulent apartments of bourgeois residents, they trace with their harmoniously aligned façades the avenues, side streets, and intersections that used to be here. At its center the explosion has destroyed even the pavement, leaving in its place a crater that is soon filled with running water from the ruptured pipes; this gutted oblong perimeter, leveled more or less by the clearing department, was then slowly transformed into a country road that was too wide, lost, uncertain, meandering between rubble-strewn plots. At this spot the black notebook includes several pages of computations concerning the relative positions of the remaining buildings—preserved by a miracle, or by chance, or by deliberate skill—as well as the sketch of an object without apparent meaning, a side view that resembles an egg cracked along its axis, or perhaps an apricot.

It looks as though this morning might be sunny, and I'll be sitting without my cane and mustache on the terrace of the Rudolph Café, facing the sea, having exchanged the dark overcoat and bowler hat for a light-weight white suit more in keeping with this place and the time of year. It will allow me all the better to pass unnoticed among the strollers and, like them, to look absentmindedly at the lively games of the pretty girls on the as yet deserted beach (why not?), when presently they will arrive for a swim in twos and threes, holding hands as they run in flocks, crying out like seagulls.

I want to take advantage of this respite to read carefully the article that must be a daily feature in the final edition of the *Globe*, the one I have just bought at the neighboring kiosk. No sooner have I opened the newspaper to the page devoted to sex crimes than I feel my face flush at the sight of a photograph, spread across three columns, of the small leather case belonging to the false doctor. I had completely forgotten this object, which now reappears—as I might have expected—at the very moment when everything, at last, seemed in more or less satisfactory, if not perfect, order.

I should have been on my guard during the idle discussion concerning the alleged virginity of the missing girls. What could there have been inside such a case? Certainly not apples! Nor sandwiches for the road (chloroformed, for that matter!) . . . It would be a mistake to shrug this off: if I am not careful, this banal sandwich story will come back to haunt me when I least expect it. As for the doctor, he will have been recognized

without difficulty: he appeared at the beginning of the inquest in the long hallway of the thermal establishment. After meeting him and exchanging a brief, anonymous greeting, I looked back in his direction, without thinking, only to note with surprise that he too had turned around, that he had even stopped walking in order to examine me at his leisure. I also stopped short, my body frozen in an awkward and twisted posture, my shoulder turned in what should have lasted no more than several seconds, but which now threatened to go on forever, if I could not find some pretext with which to end it. Indeed, we remained standing without saying anything for a very long time.

Then he asked me, in what seemed like an affectedly pleasant voice, if I needed something. I said I was looking for an exit. He seemed not to understand the meaning of my remark, simple as it was, and he continued to look at me, silently, from behind tight-fitting steel-rimmed glasses with what seemed to me to be astonishment or even solicitude: it was as if he was worried about me; puzzled as to what fate held in store for me, or in some way preoccupied with a question concerning me; no doubt he would have wished to help me, had it been in his power to do so. In the middle of his motionless, silent misgivings, he moved suddenly, as though the possibility of a solution

had suddenly occurred to him: with his free hand he unbuttoned his coat, then his jacket, and from the small pocket of his vest he withdrew a big, old-fashioned watch on a golden chain. Whatever he discovered by consulting the dial with a quick glance must no doubt have caused him to cancel the project that had been forming in his mind, because he quickly turned around; and, even while putting the watch back in its place, he resumed walking with a lively step toward the far end of the interminable hallway. Or else his gesture, and the easy alibi of checking the time, had only one purpose: a plausible ending to our awkward tête-à-tête.

At that moment, however, it occurred to me that the man must have been, quite simply, one of the musicians of the orchestra on his way to the dressing room, and that he might very well have been afraid of being late for the beginning of the rehearsal; the black attaché case therefore contained some kind of wind instrument, probably dismantled. In fact, one could already hear in the distance the intermittent sounds of a large group tuning up: flute scales or horn calls discernible against a shifting background of muted strings and percussion, while at regular intervals the voice of a soprano repeats the same short fragment of her great aria. Henceforth it is difficult for me to move on from room to room in search of the one with the wide open window overlooking the rocks, the sand, and the sea. A wooden chair with a cane seat, which

is right next to me without my having noticed it before, provides the needed excuse, fortunately: I sit down on it with ease, intending to give the situation some sober thought.

It was only then that I noticed the blood under the door, a red liquid flowing in a wide, thick, and shiny stream through the crack, where approximately half a centimeter separates the bottom of the closed door of one of the nearby rooms and the floor, then advancing toward the median zone of the corridor, to end soon enough in a small pool whose irregular outline and presence at this point reveals a slight depression in the floor that would barely be perceptible without it. A woman's shoe made of fine white leather and adorned with precious stones, no doubt artificial, is lying on its side, its high heel bathing in this viscous puddle whose color is a dark vermilion. Such a shoe must perhaps have matched a small strass bag and a tiara, worn with a particularly provocative evening gown like the ones seen at opening nights at the Opera.

Farther up, one meter and a half from the floor, the man's arm that has just dropped this shoe through the open spy window (without my knowing it?) withdraws slowly and the small movable panel turns on its hinges and slams shut, freeing the field for another consecutive but more discreet transformation: the horizontal slats of the judas

tilt slowly on their axes, revealing, in the darkness between the middle pair, two staring eyes.

Then the impersonal, toneless voice that sounds like a machine imitating speech says: Resume reading. Once more I open the black notebook and pick up where I had left off: it is the passage in which the masked criminal with the rose in his hand returns to the city, three quarters of which is in ruins, with the intention of recovering the precious case that has been left behind on the premises. But he no longer remembers where this flower comes from nor what he is expected to do with it; finally he throws it over the stone balustrade of the former bridge into the swollen and unrecognizable river. A big bird passes slowly overhead, flying upstream over the muddy waters that are carrying an odd assortment of flotsam.

A little farther on, the man picks up a black stone, apparently of volcanic origin, marked with two small indentations that look like eyes and are joined by a shiny groove, lighter in color, in the form of a V. It resembles the pattern on the head of a cobra, or a sort of scar left in the flesh by a deep gash in the shape of a shark's jaw. As for the male hand holding out the object at the time the photograph was taken, it belongs no doubt to a policeman or to some employee of the prison administration.

Aside from this stone that has fallen, who knows from where, no new element has been discovered in the last twenty-four hours that would allow the investigation to move forward. I fold the newspaper, and without further hesitation I decide to leave my hiding place: always the same exiguous room, short on comfort, lost in a section of town that is being abandoned by its last inhabitants, where an antiquated disguise will allow me to offer (to whom?) the modern and reassuring appearance, for which I am known, of a retired assassin. It is a quiet little life without problems, between the smoking stove and the ever-open window with its view of a landscape, whose coherence, day by day, is deteriorating . . . But what am I saying? And to whom? . . .

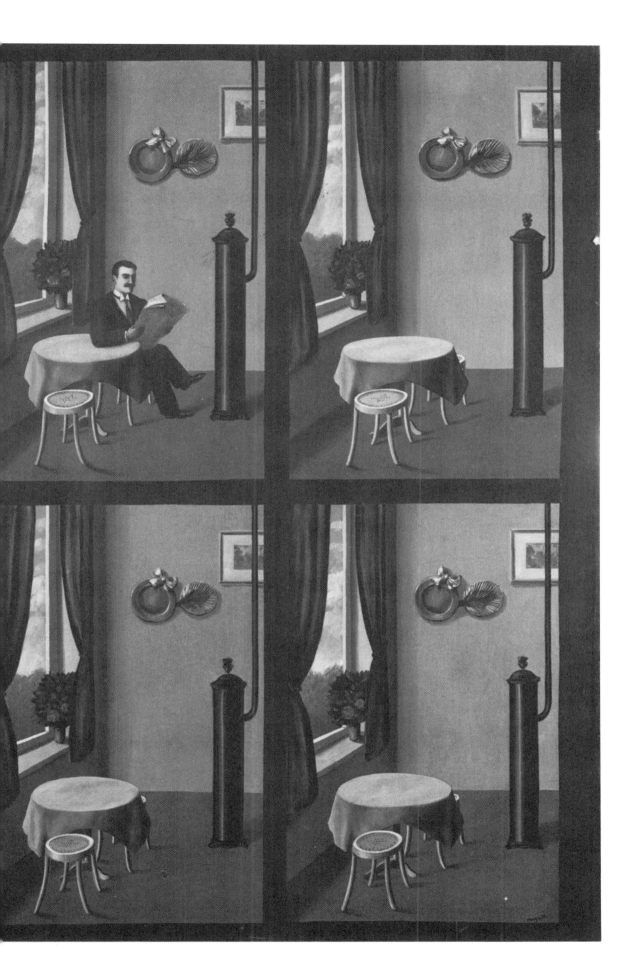

Henceforth all questions are useless. The hunt resumes once again. Already, at the far end of the long corridor, enclosed in a remote room behind parallel, vertical bars, immobile, the beautiful prisoner, as yet untouched, smiles at me inexplicably from her cage. Then the image recurs of the iron bed half-drowned in the wet sand of the long, deserted beach, exactly at the edge of the breaking wavelets. Something—I don't know what—ebbs and flows, borne by the foam. Once more something urges me out of myself toward pleasure.

THE ELUSIVE HEROINE:

AN INTERARTS ESSAY

Ben Stoltzfus

What do we make of this peculiar thing, this novel that begins and begins and begins again, moving forward, sideways, somewhere, nowhere, with its enigmatic, ever-altering characters, its blend of text and art? The old techniques of criticism obviously do not apply: curiously, they can find no purchase in the novel's many fissures because the pictures frequently contradict the written narrative.[1] Despite or because of such discontinuity and contradiction, there is a remarkable convergence of ideas and sensibility between the two men.[2] In *Écrits complets* Magritte says: "A picture and a written text may be joined, and the picture serve as an 'illustration,' whenever, in such fortunate encounters, it is conceived independently without the intention of using it as an illustration" (448). Such exactly is the "fortuitous" and "fortunate" encounter between Magritte's paintings and Robbe-Grillet's novel. The author's note on the back cover of the original edition of *La Belle Captive* invites the audience to recreate an itinerary within the moving relationships of phrase, image, and diegesis in order to generate new meaning (see Appendix B, below).

In order to "read" the dual text of *La Belle Captive*, we need to look for categories of resemblance between painting and writing. To find these categories within the two different art forms, we need to look for rhetorical analogies that will bring them together. Robbe-Grillet has done some painting, mostly collages that have been reproduced in a special issue of the review *Obliques* (16–17 [1978]: 240, plates 1–8), and he

1. A sequel to Robbe-Grillet's 1975 novel was the 1983 film, also entitled *La Belle Captive*, which he both scripted and directed. The film, although not as dialogical as the novel, alludes directly to Magritte's art.

2. See François Jost, "Le Picto-roman"; see also Jean-Pierre Vidal, "Remise à jour d'un polyptique insoupçonné de Magritte," and Georges Raillard, "Mots de passe."

readily admits that Magritte is one of his preferred painters, if not his favorite. As a young man Magritte tried his hand at writing short thrillers but was unsuccessful. The surrealist spirit that imbues so much of Magritte's work has also influenced Robbe-Grillet. Nevertheless, despite these "temperamental" affinities, the two men evolved their aesthetics independently, the one pursuing his art and the other his writing. Fortunately, the study of analogies between painting and fiction—relatively discrete art forms—allows us to analyze them outside of any historical framework.

The study of analogies between works not otherwise linked was once rejected by French comparatists of the old school; for instance, in 1921 Fernand Baldensperger denounced such a project as a futile, theoretical exercise. However, in 1973 James D. Merriman provided encouragement and grounds for comparison, stating that in "the study of the interrelations of the arts, the problem of the selection of features for comparison is of the greatest importance" (157). In recent years many interarts studies have found such "features for comparison" in a wide variety of works. Among such studies are Jacques Derrida's *Vérité en peinture* (1978), John Berger's *Ways of Seeing* (1972), Mary Ann Caws's *Eye in the Text* (1981), W. J. T. Mitchell's *Iconology: Image, Text, Ideology* (1986), Richard Wollheim's *Painting as an Art* (1987), Renée Riese Hubert's *Surrealism and the Book* (1988), Wendy Steiner's *Colors of Rhetoric: Problems in the Relation Between Modern Literature and Painting* (1982) and *Pictures of Romance* (1992), and Murray Krieger's *Ekphrasis: The Illusion of the Natural Sign* (1992), to name only a few. These studies provide critical strategies that enable us to look at writing and painting together within one discursive framework. In the case of *La Belle Captive*, the combination of writing and painting has both Robbe-Grillet's and Magritte's authorization. Insofar as many of the titles of Magritte's paintings are borrowed from literature and philosophy (*Les Liaisons dangereuses*, *Hegel's Holiday*), they provide additional comparative levels. The titles link categories of thought and aesthetics that might otherwise go unnoticed.

Any painting demonstrates the fact that in art, as in writing, a syntax is at work. Every language manufactures signs, and every syntax is a syntagmatic relationship of signs. The signs in painting, as in a written text, evolve within a coherent system. Paintings not only present objects and shapes in space but also articulate complex relationships among the elements that compose them. To read a painting independently of its "story" is to re-create or reconstruct relationships of shape, color, and design. The viewer projects order on a painterly text in the same manner that a reader interprets the rhetorical functions of a written text. Magritte's paintings have a rhetorical order and, like writing, use metaphor, metonymy, synecdoche, and irony, thus enabling us to *read* them as we would a written text. Moreover, in *La Belle Captive* Robbe-Grillet's text extends and amplifies Magritte's paintings even as Magritte's images extend and amplify Robbe-Grillet's text. The reader plays with different facets of these relationships in order to generate meaning.

Magritte's painting *The Flowers of Evil* (plate 5), although it borrows its title from Baudelaire, is an example of how metaphor works in painting: the woman is made of stone, yet the stone has the same flesh-colored tints of the rose that the naked statue is holding. Color evokes similitudes between the botanic, the mineral, and the organic, thereby establishing homologous relationships. Furthermore, whenever Magritte paints a rose, as in *The Tomb of the Wrestlers* (plate 7), *The Backfire* (plate 75), or *The Blow to the Heart* (plate 45), synecdochic, intratextual resonances evoke one or more paintings in which a rose has appeared. In *The Tomb of the Wrestlers* a red rose fills the whole room from wall to wall and from ceiling to floor. In *The Backfire* a man dressed in a tuxedo and a top hat, and holding a rose in his right hand, dominates the Paris landscape. The painted rose in *The Blow to the Heart* has a dagger on its stem instead of a thorn. Magritte based *The Backfire* on posters of the early 1900s depicting Fantômas, an underworld character featured in a popular dime-novel series; these posters show Fantômas holding a dagger, whereas Magritte's Fantômas holds a rose. Together, *The Blow to the Heart* and *The Backfire* imply that Magritte's Fantômas will stab his victims not with a dagger but with a rose. The "blow to the heart" is a metaphorical stab, and the weapon is art—an art that "subverts" natural laws by establishing "impossible" connections between people and things.

The rose is also a poetic cliché signifying love, young women, and springtime. Moreover, in Magritte's texts the rose has the same metaphorical and synecdochic role that it has in a written text, since the title *The Flowers of Evil* functions as effectively in Magritte's painting as it does in Baudelaire's poetry. However, their flowers lose their clichéd status because they are renewed and defamiliarized. Insofar as the rose "performs" the function of the dagger, *The Backfire* displays a high degree of irony. Nonetheless, the "evil" generated by Magritte's flowers, as in *The Flowers of the Abyss* (fig. 4), a painting that depicts cowbells as flowers, is merely rhetorical, and the painting is persuasive only if it convinces us to accede to a system that disrupts the familiar codes of the natural world. Magritte combines the inorganic world (clusters of cowbells) with the organic (cowbells growing as plants). This fusion of the organic and the inorganic may not be "evil" in the moral sense, but it does disrupt habitual ways of perceiving reality. Insofar as this disruption is subversive because it is antinatural— that is, against nature—some people may consider it "evil."

Another painting, *The Unexpected Answer* (plate 23), depicts a hole in a closed door. If this door were open, it would provide an entrance like the one already manifest in the hole. The door's function is being defined in a pictorial and ironic manner even as the rhetorical function of the "text" is being illustrated by juxtaposition and metonymy: the hole is to the closed door as the open door is to the wall. Although all languages are the product of culture, of *techne*, and of labor, the artist's *parole*, that is, his or her idiosyncratic use of *langue*, always deviates from cultural norms and uses. In Magritte's and Robbe-Grillet's systems, the signs oppose all codes, natural as well as social. Each man's art proposes new ways of perceiving and ordering reality. They astonish and alienate, respectively, in the surrealist and in the Brechtian sense. They produce new meaning, and they generate fresh and startling relationships between ordinary people and "familiar objects" (*Familiar Objects* [plate 61]).

Robbe-Grillet has been influenced by surrealism and shares many of its attitudes, among them the desire to shock, to scandalize, and to reorder certain ways of perceiving reality. Although some of his codes derive from surrealism, they belong essentially to postmodernism and to the nouveau roman. Nevertheless, in spite of significant differences between surrealism and postmodernism, the systems of the pictorial and the writerly overlap, making the connection between Magritte and Robbe-Grillet particularly engaging.

In "Envergure de René Magritte," André Breton reveals his own special interest in Magritte's *Belle Captive* when he says that "as captives go, there is none more desirable than one which denudes herself in total mystery." Breton sees a similarity between Magritte's "visible poetic images" and Constantin Brunner's idea of the *analogon*, a fictive process that illustrates the relationship between referential reality and its visionary counterpart. Although there is no woman in Magritte's painting, Breton alludes to her implied presence in the painting's title. The painting (title and image) is the *analogon* between immediate perception and metaphorical reality. George H. Bauer, in "The Robbe-Grillet/Magritte AV Frame; or, The Case of *La Belle Captive*," refers to that erotic center of the novel where a beautiful woman is subjugated or held prisoner (23).

Whenever two different art forms come together or are compared, questions of methodology inevitably arise. Ulrich Weisstein, in "Literature and the Visual Arts," lists sixteen possible types of linkage based on structural relationships between painting and writing. Of interest to us is category 15, in which paintings "exist in a literary context without being outright illustrations" (261). The corollary of this statement, as it applies to *La Belle Captive*, is that the narrative also exists in a painterly context without being an outright commentary on the paintings. The pictures and the text, although they reflect each other, albeit imperfectly, are essentially commentaries on themselves and on the nature of reflexive art. Together they foreground the language of art—a language that devalues mimesis while stressing the nature of the creative process. Derrida's *Glas* generates Valerio Adami's drawing *Étude pour un dessin d'après Glas* (one of two surfaces of a serigraph, double-faced object), which in turn generates portions of Derrida's *Vérité en peinture*. In similar fashion, *La Belle Captive* (the painting [plate 27]) generates *La Belle Captive* (the text), both of which educe the present discourse. *La Belle Captive* invites the reader to fill and fulfill the oscillating field between word and image. Each operational field (*le champ opératoire*) reflects the other as the reader creates meaning by reacting to the magnetic forces that alternately attract and repel the two texts. They are like the negatively and positively charged poles that Breton refers to in his surrealist manifestos, even as the reader provides the current that sends the vital spark arcing between the two. In *La Vérité en peinture*, Derrida comments apropos Adami's drawing:

> 'X. An almost perfect chiasma
> of two texts facing each other:
> a gallery and a writing method

that keep each other in view and
lose each other. The pictures are
written and that(he) which(who)
writes sees itself(himself) being
looked at by the painter.

(173)

Whenever we react to a painting with the intention of verbalizing its form or its content, we begin a process of interpretation. To look at a picture is, in essence, to make it speak. In this sense sight occupies a privileged role because without it the painting as a text cannot exist. Sight is a pre-text. Like the stone in *The Castle of the Pyrenees* (plate 1), it is an engendering force. Whether the object in a picture is a stone, an egg, or a cowbell, sight is necessary for the realization of its potential. The eye, of course, is the organ of sight. Behind every eye there is vision, and behind every reading of a picture there is an intention. Insofar as every painting is primarily a visual text, sight becomes a metaphor of intention. If beauty exists, it exists in the eye of the beholder. Only sight can generate a beautiful captive.

In reading a picture, we may also write its meaning, thus unveiling the intention of the eye's vision. When we write the picture's meaning, we unveil two intentions: the picture's and the viewer's. However, in order to communicate this dual intention we have to use language. But language—the sign system may belong to painting or to writing—has its own reality. Insofar as the signifier is never the signified, but only an element in the sign system, language is removed from the reality about which it speaks. There is the reality of the signified and the reality of the signifier. Insofar as reflexive language foregrounds the signifier at the expense of the signified, it performs a dual role: it veils and it unveils. For example, the painting entitled *The Central Story* (plate 37), like language, obscures in order to reveal. The cloth veils the head of the woman, but in doing so it unveils something else. In obscuring the face of reality, language reveals itself, thereby becoming an object in its own right. It calls attention to itself. This foregrounding of language makes it palpable. It is the body of the text—the beautiful captive to which Magritte, Breton, and Robbe-Grillet allude.

Nonetheless, even though the body is palpable, the invisible reality that lurks behind every painting is sight. The painting entitled *The False Mirror* (plate 31) depicts an eye reflecting a blue sky and white clouds. There is a black hole (the pupil) in the middle of the painting. What does it signify? This black hole, this pupil, is a point of contact. It communicates with the seer and the seen, with the inside and the outside, thereby setting up a dialectical exchange between the two. The white clouds and blue sky are in the eye and in the sky, even as the painting combines the seer and the seen. Like the veil covering the woman's head, the black pupil connotes absence because a hole is the equivalent of nothing. In *The Central Story*, the cloth covering makes the woman's face disappear, but in obscuring the face it suggests its presence. The black hole in the eye may paint the void, but the concept "void" or "absence" nevertheless implies and can be contrasted with the idea of "presence." The disappearance of the woman's face, like the black hole in the eye, is a form of abduction: the artist has taken something away. The beautiful captive, although present in some of Magritte's titles, is also always absent from these paintings. Like the head of the woman behind the cloth, the beautiful captive is invisible. It is as though she too has been abducted. Paradoxically, this absence, this invisibility, depends on sight, since the eye "sees" what is not there. The invisible conjures the visible. Absence suggests the possibility of presence. Such a dialectic dramatizes not only disappearance but also the process of seeing. In effect, it organizes a theater of sight. The reader is simultaneously seeing and reading the paintings.

There is also, of course, the body of the written text. Reading and seeing put this body on stage—this is the meaning of "foregrounding"—where the beautiful captive performs her assigned role. In dramatizing painting and language, Magritte and Robbe-Grillet are also staging thought. "Writing," says Magritte, "is the invisible description of thought while painting is its visible description" (*EC* 686). The dual script reveals clearly that sight can be written and that writing can be seen: Robbe-Grillet's text writes Magritte's pictures, and Magritte's pictures "see" Robbe-Grillet's text. Each one frames the other, even as the reader becomes the mediator between the two alternating and reversible processes. But the frame of each picture as well as the limits of the novel are artificial barriers. Like a Möbius strip they overlap, containing each other in their reversibility. (Magritte's painting *The Empty Picture Frame* [or *Blood-letting*] further reinforces the idea of nothingness and abduction.)

Writing and seeing are thus two complementary aspects of the self. Jasper Johns's painting *The Critic Sees* depicts this slippage of emphasis and meaning. A pair of eyeglasses frames two mouths instead of eyes—mouths that seem to be articulating what "the critic sees." Language mirrors this dual process, but language—particularly encratic language—also mirrors the duality of the self. Since we are all products of *langue* and *parole*, we strive to assert an authenticity against the weight of ideology. *La Belle Captive*'s narrator, reading about the criminal in the newspaper, reads a description of a composite image of a man who has no identity except the clichéd identity of "everyman." He is the bowler-hatted man whose crimes and transgressions are reported every day in the newspaper (*Le Globe*) in the clichéd language that renders all such accounts palatable. This encratic language mirrors a collective identity in which the reader recognizes a potential self, a double, whose dreams and obsessions belong to society's collective unconscious.

Magritte's and Robbe-Grillet's *parole* both sees and speaks the world. The paintings and the text illumine each other. Similarly, Rimbaud's *Illuminations* are aptly titled, since the author is the "seer" (*le voyant*) who records his visions. His illuminations are his text, his poems—in short, writing. Reflexive writing may veil the object, but it unveils perception. Such an *écriture* depends on a process that cannot be described except through the object. Language is objectified. Not only does it describe things, but it itself becomes a thing, like those paintings that refuse to imitate nature but instead speak of their existence as objects. This foregrounding of language dramatizes its corporeality, but there is also an absence and a void—the black pupil in *The False Mirror*. Hence the duality and the simultaneity of presence and absence, as in the novel *La Jalousie*, in which an "absent" husband objectifies his jealousy in things. Hence also the mirrors, the doubles, the gaps, and the chiasmas that are the reflections of the body of the text and of another self: an I, perhaps, that sees itself in the mirror of the cell (*Not to Be Reproduced* [plate 24]) but does not recognize itself; or the I that sees a resemblance between the self and the man at the other end of the labyrinthine corridor, that is, the self formed by *langue*—trapped in the labyrinth of encratic language. This self that ideology strives to mold in its own image exists as in a dream. This is the nightmare that structures the diegesis of the film *La Belle Captive*.

In short, the body of the text, the locus of my sight, is the site of an inscription, the pre-text of my intentionality, and the writing of the picture text. Sight constructs the visible, and writing is its re-creation. The body of the text—the beautiful captive—contains the meaning of the message. Seeing and reading are the progressive unveiling of her body. She is a presence and an absence, simultaneously. As a process of unveiling, the language of art renders the invisible visible. "The central story" is in the lifting of the cloth. Magritte's and Robbe-Grillet's discourse reveals the body, the metaphor of an idea mediated by sight. Their texts unveil the hidden face of desire whose body strives "toward pleasure" (*Toward Pleasure* [plate 69]) as an antidote to death (the void) and repression (ideology). This is why our narrator abducts his victim and carries her to the secret room where the textual and sexual experiments take place.

Dream, pleasure, and narration, with the reader's constant help, combine image and word into a piece of fiction that mimes the story of telling. This novel's oneiric quality allows it to function in the present, but it evokes a mythical reality that is full of historical connotations. Moreover, if sex is the motor of production and consumption, then we need to rethink the premises of world economics along principles that explain humankind's constant striving for pleasure. Our energies and dependencies are forces generated by desire. Desire plays with language and with reality in order to open the doors of opportunity. Beyond every door is a potential "captive," an "unexpected answer," a new beginning, and an invitation to the "art of living" (fig. 8).

We have already discussed the metaphorical and synecdochic role of the rose. Another such object is the valise, which invites the reader to open its lid as one would open the covers of a book. The reader cannot know what is inside until he or she opens the book to inspect its contents. However, inspecting the contents may not be enough, since it is in playing with them that the reader generates meaning. Whether spectacle or representation, pleasure comes from rearranging the contents.

The written and visual diegesis emphasizes the reader's production of meaning as a source of pleasure (*jouissance*). Wolfgang Iser argues that a literary work is actualized only when the reader supplies that portion of it that is implied but not written, that the "concretization" of a text requires the participation of the reader's imagination, that his or her reading uncovers the "unformulated part" of the text's "intention" (274–94). If the production of meaning and pleasure are part of the text's "intention," which the titles of the paintings and the narrative allude to so forcefully (*The Pleasure Principle* [plate 50], *Toward Pleasure* [plate 69], *Pleasure* [plate 64]), then the reader has to join the two sign systems. She or he must not only determine the poetic significance of each text but must also bring them together in such a way as to make sense out of the whole.

For Iser, the role of the reader is to fill in the gaps in the written text. However, because *La Belle Captive* is composed of two simultaneous texts (painting and writing) that are activated by the reader's eye, the gaps in it are more complex than the ones Iser refers to, and the demands on the reader have multiplied. The so-called objective text that Walker Gibson, Gerald Prince, and Michael Riffaterre believe in has disappeared. There can be only an approximation of a text. First, there are the gaps in the ordering of Magritte's paintings; then there are the gaps in the written narrative; and finally there is the biggest gap of all—that unwritten and unpainted portion between the two that requires an entirely new strategy of re-creation. The attempt to combine the two art forms into a coherent whole requires a new repertoire of interpretive devices and "productive" endeavors that depend on the reader's willingness to "read" the pictures and the written text simultaneously. In essence, the reader makes the pictures "speak" and the text "see." To combine Magritte's and Robbe-Grillet's codes is thus to become a "superreader," but with a difference. Whereas Riffaterre, in his essay on Baudelaire's "Les Chats," recognizes the role of the "informed" reader in deciphering the subliminal intentions of the text—intentions that transcend the limitations of its linguistic syntagmas—he still believes that literary meaning resides in the language of the text. The two textual codes of *La Belle Captive* are so "indeterminate," so fragmented, so contradictory, and so "open" that the reader either refuses to play the game or, if inspired, rises to the challenge. This ideal reader no longer "consumes" the text and discards it as one would a best-seller; rather, she or he produces the text. Titles of paintings such as *Toward Pleasure*, *Pleasure*, and *The Master of the Revels* (the French title is *Le Maître du plaisir* [plate 63]), in association with *Anne-Marie and the Rose* (the last painting in the book [plate 77]) and the accelerating thrust of the written narrative, move toward bliss (*jouissance*) the way intercourse strives for climax. If the reader plays with the body of the text, the game engenders a productive relationship. But the production of meaning, as a human activity, necessarily involves the text and the audience. However, a text such as *La Belle Captive* requires a more active and more ingenious audience response than any yet proposed.

REPRESENTATION

Although Magritte's and Robbe-Grillet's titles evoke the image of a captive woman, her "representation" is problematic (plate 60). *The Beautiful Captive*, as a title, is essentially a metaphor enabling art to make a statement about itself. The "beautiful captive" is thus not a flesh-and-blood woman but a pictorial and writerly event. Magritte's *Beautiful Captive* (plate 27) dramatizes the artistic process as much as Robbe-Grillet's discourse subverts accepted models of writing; or, if you will, Robbe-Grillet's fiction dramatizes the writing process even as Magritte's discourse devalues reality. This change of status within the fictive body—a status that opposes the tenets of classic realism to the poetics of postmodernism—allows for bifurcations and metamorphoses that generate unusual narrative displacements.

These narrative displacements focus on the woman's body as a metaphor for the painterly and artistic process. A woman's body is, in fact, central to Magritte's work, from his earliest cubistic paintings—*Women and Flowers* (1920), *Three Nudes in an Interior* (1923 [fig. 9]), and *Woman* (1923)—to *The Beautiful Captive* seascape he painted just before his death. In such pictures as *Bather* (1925 [fig. 10]), *The Importance of Marvels* (1927), *Black Magic* (1933 or 1934 [plate 56]), *Bather Between Light and Darkness* (1935 or 1936 [fig. 11]), *The Flowers of Evil* (1946 [plate 5]), *Olympia* (1947), and so on, the images of woman and seascape are closely linked. The woman is in the foreground and the sea is in the background. The window or opening through which the seascape is visible in *Bather* becomes the painting of a seascape hanging on the wall in *Bather Between Light and Darkness*. Moreover (the connection is important for the 1947 version of *The Beautiful Captive* [fig. 1]), the painting has the transparency of a glass window. The ornamental sphere situated behind the reclining woman of *Bather* obscures the right breast of the reclining woman of *Bather Between Light and Darkness*. The similarities in theme and composition between the two paintings are striking. Just as striking, in two seascape versions of *The Beautiful Captive* (plate 27 and fig. 1) the reclining women have been replaced with an easel holding a canvas that duplicates the seascape. There is an inevitable association between the title, the woman, and the painting(s). Furthermore, the ornamental sphere of *Bather* and *Bather Between Light and Darkness* reappears as the giant sphere on the beach in *The Beautiful Captive* (plate 27). Spherical objects, whether breasts, balls, balloons, bells (the *grelots*), or apples, although they may represent bourgeois complacence or the ideal of absolute textual reflexivity, nonetheless also signify woman and, by extension, desire. *The Happy Life* depicts a round transparent fruit containing a woman in the fetal position.

Magritte dramatizes the analogies between round objects and women in the painting *The Beautiful World* (fig. 12). In many ways it resembles *The Beautiful Captive*: the title has a familiar ring to it, the two skies look alike, and the curtains are similar. However, the sphere on the beach has become an apple, and the horizon is the edge of a tabletop. In yet another painting, *Wasted Effort*, the sky, clouds, and curtains resemble those of *The Beautiful World*, but the apple has now metamorphosed into one of Magritte's ubiquitous cowbells. It would be easy to extend the analogies and comment on the permutations of woman, bell, apple, sphere, and so on. These permutations reflect an alchemical, psychoanalytical, and symbolic transmutation of matter that allows one thing to signify another in an elaborate network of cross-references that includes eggs, roses, stones, and women. In the ironic portrait *Mona Lisa* (fig. 13), the head and face of the Mona Lisa have been replaced with a cowbell. There is perhaps no longer any doubt as to the slippage of signifiers and the congruence of woman with spherical objects, with the artistic process, or with desire.

Magritte was also aware of the latent analogies between objects and words, and he exploited the slippages of meaning between things, names, and ideas—between the sign, the signifier, and the signified. For instance, *The Voice of the Winds* depicts three giant *grelots* like silver spaceships, floating in the blue sky above a green landscape. Says Magritte: "I preferred to believe that the iron bells hanging from our fine horses' necks grew there like poisonous plants on the edge of precipices" (*EC* 109). The materialization of this preference, *The Flowers of the Abyss* (fig. 4), shows a rocky chasm in which leaves and bellflowers are growing. A slight turn of the screw, as Henry James would have phrased it, transforms *The Flowers of the Abyss* into *The Flowers of Evil*, a sisterly painting whose title suggests a transference of meaning to the flesh-colored woman-statue holding the flesh-colored rose (plate 5). The "living" statue, like the sphere on the beach in *The Beautiful Captive*, is set against a backdrop of sea and sky, framed by the red curtains, thus providing yet another variation dramatizing artistic magic.

Although the title *The Beautiful Captive* connotes woman, the painting itself denotes the painterly process and the ambiguities of perception. In *Representation* (plate 60), Magritte calls our attention, as he did in *The Treachery of Images* (fig. 14), to the fact that the image is not a person or an object but a representation of one. The "representation" of a woman's body, from the thighs to the breasts, has an additional ambiguity in that the picture, whose contours are framed as body contours, looks like a mirror image. Yet the mirror image is no more real than its painted counterpart. The acute realism of the painting and of the title is subverted. It is the representation of a painting, not a woman's body. Nevertheless, the generative force behind this painting, and all the other "beautiful captives," is woman. She is—or, rather, they are—*The Magician's Accomplices* (plate 6), that is, the artist's helpers. *The Magician* was the title of a film project conceived by Robbe-Grillet in 1964 and published in *Obliques* (16–17: 259–61). The text focuses on different interlocking levels concerning the making of a film, the actors' fictitious roles, their real lives, and the reciprocal influences of the real and the imaginary. The artist is the magician who transforms life into art and vice versa.

A QUANTUM LEAP

Magritte defies the law of gravity whenever he paints a rock floating in the air like a cloud, as in *The Battle of the Argonne* (fig. 2). Space is abolished when, in denying perspective or in fusing the inside and the outside, he dissolves the bipolarity of "here" and "there," as in *The Human Condition I* (fig. 15). He stops or accelerates time and duration when he juxtaposes a daylight sky with a nighttime landscape, as in the lit windows, streetlamps, and evening shadows of *The Dominion of Light* (fig. 16). Magritte paints irreconcilable simultaneous events as observed from a single point of view, thus disrupting our sense of gravity and space-time.

Suzi Gablik believes that this plural significance of experience corresponds to Einstein's theory of relativity (123). Relativity has in fact destroyed our view of the universe as static and predictable. Whereas Newtonian mechanics asserted that events could be ordered in time independently of their location in space, relativity theory and quantum mechanics state that absolute rest and absolute motion cannot exist and that everything in the physical world is relative to an observer. The Euclidean world was precise, determinate, and invariable. Einstein's universe is dynamic: everything is in the process of becoming. Magritte's images and Robbe-Grillet's fiction show unusual sensitivity to these changes in scientific theory: events that should be separate in time are painted or described simultaneously, physical laws are reversed in ways that subvert our acquired, commonsense views of reality, substances are altered, and natural phenomena are modified.

Magritte's paradoxical juxtapositions, combining precise visual detail with fantastic or "impossible" representations, correspond to Robbe-Grillet's transpositions, dislocations, and disruptions of nineteenth-century narrative realism. As Robbe-Grillet comments:

> The nineteenth-century narrative wanted to describe a historical or pseudo-historical reality, whereas the modern narrative parades its power of invention; . . . the Balzacian narrative describes a closed reality; the modern narrative believes that it evolves continuously, and in such a way that this reality will never be finished, nor can the work itself circumscribe it. The work will be a permanent interrogation that will never have a definitive ending.
>
> ("Autour du film *L'Immortelle*" 108)

In "Spatial Form in Modern Literature," Joseph Frank states that in art and literature, one naturally spatial and the other naturally temporal, there has been an identical evolution of aesthetic form in the twentieth century. In fact, both arts have moved to overcome the time elements involved in their perception because both are rooted in the same spiritual and emotional climate. This shift in perception from a stable and predictable world to a world governed by Heisenberg's "uncertainty principle," as it affects the sensibility of many artists, affects the forms they create in every medium. Contemporary artists accentuate the inherent spatiality of the plastic arts by removing all traces of time value. Since postmodern writing is nonnaturalistic, we can say that it too is moving in the direction of increased spatiality. In Robbe-Grillet's works, simultaneity, circularity, and discontinuity are an indication of this trend. To illustrate a novel with Magritte's paintings is to emphasize further the spatiality of writing.

Frank explains all this with Ezra Pound's definition of an image as "that which presents an intellectual and emotional complex in an instant of time." An image is not a pictorial reproduction, says Frank, but a unification of disparate ideas and emotions into a "complex" that is presented spatially. Insofar as an image of this kind has an immediate impact on the reader's sensibility, it does not proceed discursively but elicits a sense of sudden liberation from time and space (226). Magritte's art and Robbe-Grillet's fiction fit Pound's and Frank's definitions perfectly. Each of Magritte's paintings is a "complex." Robbe-Grillet also abolishes any objective, causal progression in time by juxtaposing the past and the present. In *La Jalousie* the past and the present are seen spatially, and the husband's fear and passion are objectified as the stain of a centipede on a dining room wall. All sense of depth has vanished, and everything exists in a timeless present—*maintenant* (now)—the word with which the novel begins.

Even as Robbe-Grillet's fiction has moved toward the painterly, many of Magritte's titles were designed to evoke literary antecedents with references to Baudelaire (*The Flowers of Evil* [plate 5]), Poe (*The Domain of Arnheim* [plate 10]), Laclos (*Les Liaisons dangereuses*), Sade (*Philosophy in the Boudoir* [plate 29]), Lautréamont, and the surrealists. Like Lautréamont, who describes fleas as large as elephants, Magritte creates a new and different world order that rivals Genesis: living statues, mermaids, bird-leaves, and so on. *Collective Invention* (plate 48), for example, is a 1934 painting depicting an unusual mermaid, one with a woman's legs and a fish's head and torso. In 1938 an edition of Lautréamont's *Oeuvres complètes* was published. Breton wrote the introduction to the collection, which was illustrated by many surrealist works, including Magritte's own painting *The Rape* (fig. 17). In 1948 another edition of *Les Chants de Maldoror* was published, with seventy-seven illustrations done entirely by Magritte. Robbe-Grillet's publication of *La Belle Captive* links him, by extension, to these earlier editions and to surrealism.[3] Says Magritte:

> Lautréamont's image, for example, the chance encounter on a dissecting table of an umbrella and a sewing machine, could also be described in a manner of speaking as symbolic: of disorder, since things are not where they are supposed to be. But to say that is to fail to grasp the inherent poetry and mystery of the image.

> (*EC* 647)

Although Magritte emphasizes the mystery of things, most of the surrealists preferred the surprise elicited by chance encounters or the juxtaposition of objects that

---

3. See also Ben Stoltzfus, "Alain Robbe-Grillet and Surrealism." This is the first critical study linking Robbe-Grillet with surrealism.

appear unrelated but that, as with the sewing machine and the umbrella, produce a strong affective charge. Certain objects are not where they should be, and it is these Freudian displacements, dramatizations, and condensations that defamiliarize the reality of Magritte's representations.

THE GENERATIVE STONE

Magritte's art commingles the real and the unreal. The floating rocks and flying stones belong to an imaginary world whose realism and intensity rival the natural one we are familiar with. *La Belle Captive* opens with the following sentence: "It begins with a stone falling, in the silence, vertically, immobile. It is falling from a great height, a meteor, a massive, compact, oblong block of rock, like a giant egg with a pocked, uneven surface" (above, 15). *The Castle of the Pyrenees* (plate 1) depicts the sea, the sky, the rock hovering above the waves, and the castle on the rock. The French expression "Faire des châteaux en Espagne" means to daydream. The title of this painting relates it to the dream motif of the surrealists, whose aesthetic doctrine was based on the synthesis of dream and reality and on a union of the intellect and the senses. The Pyrenees are as natural and formidable a barrier between France and Spain as the barrier between reason (France is the nation of Descartes) and passion (Spain is the country of *pundonor*, the code of absolute honor), as the difference between being awake and dreaming.

An art that incorporates elements of both dream and reality goes a long way toward resolving the contradictions between the two. The visual impact of a painting that nullifies gravity contributes to a breakdown in the realism of the real. Magritte's rock never hits the water, but Robbe-Grillet's text plunges us and the rock into the dream world of the surreal below the surface of the waves. By beginning his novel with *The Castle of the Pyrenees*, Robbe-Grillet invokes the oneiric, thereby enabling the reader to cross the border between the two landscapes and the two realities. In *Pour un nouveau roman* Robbe-Grillet says, "this *waking dream* could simply be *art*, of which sleep, it is true, sometimes gives us fragments, but which only a conscious effort allows us to reassemble" (88).

Ironically, Magritte's painting *The Alarm Clock* suggests that these dreams are intended not to put us to sleep but to wake us up. Nevertheless, *The Castle of the Pyrenees* juxtaposes objects as dream elements that easily fit Freud's categories of displacement and condensation: displacing an object from its natural surroundings (the castle is not in the Pyrenees, despite the title) and joining things in unusual contexts (the castle on the rock). An inverse relationship in size exists between the castle and the rock, since "experience" dictates that big castles are built from stones of a smaller size than the one depicted in the painting. Its title and its contents combine to signify "dream." For Robbe-Grillet's text, it is the "beginning," the writing of a dream engendered by the falling stone. It is a stone suspended above the sea. Robbe-Grillet's decision to begin his narrative with this painting is significant in many ways: the stone that looks like an egg is a generative cell, the beginning of the *writing process* whose rhythm (*rythmos*), says

Derrida in *La Vérité en peinture*, signifies simultaneously "the cadence of an *écriture* and the undulation of the waves" (183).

The undulating sea (*la mer*, *la mère*—the sea, the mother) contains not only the rhythm of writing but the rhythm of a dream (the text) where women (Vanessa, her mother, the female student, the mermaid, the beautiful captive) embody different manifestations of the individual as well as the collective unconscious. The stone falls into the sea, thus generating the text, and the dream begins. Reality has gone topsy-turvy. The giant inverted head of the *Portrait of a Woman* (plate 2) looks into a room where two small men are dwarfed by an enormous rock. We are moving into "the invisible world" of the dream in which rocks become weightless, or become birds, as in *The Idol* (plate 13), or become flesh, as in *The Flowers of Evil* (plate 5).

In addition to the intertextual allusion to Baudelaire's book of poems of the title, the woman statue in *The Flowers of Evil*, who is both flesh and stone, is a quasi-literal transcription of a line from Baudelaire's poem "La Beauté": "I am beautiful, oh mortal souls! as a dream of stone." The dream motif (not to mention the stone) so dear to the surrealists relates this quotation and this painting to *The Castle of the Pyrenees* and to *The Cape of Storms* (plate 49), which depicts a man sleeping inside an oblong box. Beyond the box on a sienna plain is a huge stone. Indeed, *The Cape of Storms* depicts a land of dreams.

The surrealists wished not only to cross the border of the Pyrenees, so to speak—to venture from dream to reality—but also to resolve the contradictions. Magritte achieves this synthesis in *In Praise of the Dialectic* (plate 19), which presents two synchronous views of the inside and the outside of a room, a window, and a building. In reproducing Magritte's painting of *The Night Owl* (plate 17), Robbe-Grillet emphasizes the oneiric dimension of this conscious quest for simultaneity. The stone is the beginning of the dream of man.

Magritte, like Robbe-Grillet, also stresses the consciously constructed elements of the artistic process. Louis Scutenaire quotes Magritte as follows:

> We would like the domain of the dream to be respectable—but our works are not oneiric, *on the contrary*. When we refer to "the dream" it is to a very different kind of dream than the ones we have while sleeping. On the contrary, it concerns *voluntary dreams*—dreams that are not at all vague, like the feelings we might have when escaping into a day-dream.
>
> (106)

Let us return to *The Castle of the Pyrenees* and the falling stone. We sense that it has all the solidity and permanence of a consciously constructed work of art. In *The Sacred and the Profane*, Mircea Eliade notes that stones symbolize power, hardness, and permanence, and he stresses their *hierophany*, their value as sacred objects (155). The black rock in Mecca is sacred to millions of Muslims even as the rock of Jerusalem is said to be the "Foundation Stone of the Earth, that is, the navel of the Earth, because it is from there that the whole Earth unfolded" (44). The irreducibility of stones, says Eliade, reveals to humankind an absolute existence that is beyond time, invulnerable to becoming. It is the irruption of the sacred into the world.

It is this absolute irreducibility of stone that both Magritte and Robbe-Grillet question. Instead of remaining constant, Magritte's stones begin to change as they assume life and metamorphose into a bird, a woman, an egg, and so on. Magritte's stones are endowed with properties that contradict the essence Eliade attributes to them. From sacred, they have become profane.

Although profane, the stone retains a formidable generative power. Harry Torczyner quotes a letter to Magritte from the physicist Albert V. Baez, who notes that the rock in *The Castle of the Pyrenees* dramatizes space, time, and matter in suspended animation. Even though familiarity with the force of gravity may cause us to ignore it, because it is commonplace, in this painting, says Baez, it becomes "powerful and awesome" (99). Instead of exploiting the rock's "sacred" potential, Magritte and Robbe-Grillet explore its pulsive forces. The stone, in denying its clichéd characteristic—mass—undermines the basic processes of definition. It calls into question the laws and expectations of gravity, language, and culture. This, as we shall see, is a radical and well-aimed attack on bourgeois ideology and on the myth of the "natural." By defying the laws of nature, this rock asserts a new mystery and thereby manifests a new reality.

The stone is now a generative cell, an egg—the beginning. Not the Word, but the Image. And the image speaks. The reader sees, but he or she also listens. The stone's oval shape is no accident, and its resemblance to an egg is deliberate. There is more. *The Domain of Arnheim* (plate 10), although alluding to Edgar Allan Poe's work, depicts a mountain rising to a bird's head, eye, and beak. The ridge and crags, partly covered with snow, are the bird's spread wings. A crescent moon hovers in the pale blue sky above the bird. In the foreground, on a stone wall, is a nest containing three eggs. The whiteness of the eggs matches the whiteness of the moon. The moon's incipient roundness relates to the oval shape of the eggs. The slippage between animal, mineral, and vegetable—the nest—is constant. The painting also suggests a connection between lunar cycles and biological forces, an evolutionary symbiosis between the organic and the inorganic, between Anne-Marie as mythic goddess (in *Anne-Marie and the Rose* [plate 77]) and this bird-mountain that has come to life under the sign of the crescent moon. The painting seems to imply that this unusual species has laid the eggs, a conclusion that is consonant with the oval shape of the rock in *The Castle of the Pyrenees* and Robbe-Grillet's description of its egglike form. Robbe-Grillet himself, in "*L'Eden et après*: Début pour un ciné-roman," stresses the fact that woman, as a mythical object, maintains a secret rapport with nature's rhythms, reproductive forces, and lunar cycles (192).

La Belle Captive begins with a rock that is like an egg; or it is a mountain that lays eggs—like the parthenogenetic one that explodes in a ball of fire, giving birth to the

Phoenix. In turn, the Phoenix, before being consumed, lays the egg from which the "mythic" twins David and Vanessa are born. Robbe-Grillet's egg, on one level, deflates mythology by parodying its mythic content. On another level, the eggs call attention to the productive cells of language as the narrative source. These cells, whether images, things, or colors (*Projet pour une révolution à New York* was generated from a door and the color red), split, change, and multiply, becoming in time the body of the text. Meanwhile, they function as coded units of information, like the biological cells from which they derive their name. They contain mythic lore, cultural images, social stereotypes, religious mysticism, and tales of the fantastic. The legend of the mermaid is one such mythic image that Magritte parodies in *Collective Invention* (plate 48). Likewise, Robbe-Grillet imagines a sirenlike Vanessa, a woman whose body has been brought to the surface in a fisherman's net.

In *Magritte, poète visible*, Philippe Roberts-Jones says that the painter was fascinated not only by stones and mermaids but by the relationship between stone and flesh (25). *The Flowers of Evil* (plate 5) is the epitome of such a marriage between the animate and inanimate. Says Magritte: "The flesh statue of a young woman is holding in her hand a rose made of flesh. Her other hand is leaning against a rock. The curtains open onto the sea and a summer sky" (*EC* 175). Even more, *The Flowers of Evil* modifies the accepted relationships between people and objects. The woman in the painting has a sensuous reality, but she is made of stone; she has the blank eyes of a statue, but she looks alive. This movement back and forth between the real and the unreal, between hardness and softness, between warm flesh and cold stone, sets up resonances that reverberate throughout Magritte's work. He has upset our normal associative processes.[4]

In a manner not unlike Magritte's, Robbe-Grillet endows "stabbed mannequins" with life; seaweed is transformed into long blonde tresses, a seashell becomes a vagina, and stones, like eggs, have an innate reproductive force: the stone in *The Castle of the Pyrenees* is the generative cell for *La Belle Captive*. This stone or rock appears in the first three illustrations in the book, a significant triple (some would say "sacred") sequence: *The Castle of the Pyrenees*, *Portrait of a Woman*, and *The Invisible World* (plates 1–3). In *Portrait of a Woman* the egg-shaped rock is the size of the woman's head. In *The Invisible World* the same giant rock is set on the floor inside a room, obscuring parts of the balcony and the sea. The seascape (the sea and stormy sky) is visible through the open French doors. The fourth illustration is the all-important *The Murderer Threatened*, followed again in the fifth with a rocklike protrusion and the statue woman in *The Flowers of Evil* (plates 4–5). The first three rocks not only look like eggs but soon begin to fly like birds, as in the flying stone bird depicted in *The Idol* (plate 13). *The Domain of*

---

4. Says Magritte: "A stone statue, entirely of flesh, may seem immoral because it is too carnal, not to mention the flesh flower that the statue holds in its hand" (*EC* 260). For an interesting treatment of the generative interrelationships between stones, woman, and rose, see Vidal, "Remise à jour," 221–24.

Arnheim (plate 10) suggests that this bird of stone is capable of laying eggs or that the mountain protects these eggs, as a bird mother would. Moreover, this rock, which appears frequently when women are present, eventually becomes a woman-statue. It should not surprise us, then, that in 1947 Magritte incorporated the rock into another version of *The Beautiful Captive* (fig. 1).

This version, like the others, depicts an easel and a "transparent" painting (framed this time, as in *Bather Between Light and Darkness* [fig. 11]). The sea and the sky coincide (as they did in the 1967 version of *The Beautiful Captive* [plate 27]) with the realism of the seascape on the canvas. However, instead of curtains we have a flaming tuba—a tuba that appears in other paintings: *The Flood*, in which a naked woman is leaning on the tuba; in *Threatening Weather* (plate 73), in which the tuba, next to the torso of a woman and a chair, is suspended in the sky over a seascape; and in *The Ladder of Fire* (plate 14), in which, inside a room, the tuba, a chair, and a piece of paper are burning. In *The Flood* and in *Threatening Weather*, the nonburning tuba is next to the body of a woman. In *The Beautiful Captive* (fig. 1), as in *The Ladder of Fire*, there is no woman, but the burning tuba, with its image of fire, alludes directly to her.

Magritte links fire with pleasure: "The astonishing discovery of fire, thanks to the rubbing together of two bodies, reminds us of the physical mechanism of pleasure" (*EC* 259). Moreover, says Suzi Gablik, in her study of Magritte, "fire is always an image of primary sexuality" (98). Indeed, the frame of the transparent picture links fire, the stone, and the tuba in a fundamental way, particularly when we recall that the title of one of the "stone" pictures is *The Invisible World* (plate 3). Since the flames of the burning tuba cast a reflection on the canvas (or is it the seascape?), we conceive the idea that the canvas is both a pane of glass that allows the viewer to see through reality and a painting as a metaphorical window on reality. Such art synthesizes the inner world of the artist's intentions with the outer world that is visible through "the window." Different but corresponding levels of perception merge on the surface of a reflected (or is it a transparent?) consciousness. If we look closely, the burning reflection illumines the breasts and body of a naked woman. "My paintings," says Magritte, "are visible thoughts" (*EC* 537).

THE BEAUTIFUL CAPTIVE

Who is the beautiful captive? At the risk of getting ahead of myself, I will suggest that *The Beautiful Captive* (plate 27) and the many variations of this painting—such as *The Beautiful World* (fig. 12), *The Human Condition I* (fig. 15), *The Human Condition II* (plate 66), *Plagiarism*, and all the other intermeshing pictorial spinoffs—represent the artist's exploration of a triple reality: the subject, the object, and the language that brings them together. The "beautiful captive" is therefore the perceiving self, the reality we perceive, and the metalanguage that describes and determines that reality. Although "she" has a triple reality, like the Deity, perhaps her greatest attribute is to be "the body of the text" (or of the picture)—that fictive body that only art can render visible.[5]

In *Art and Illusion* E. H. Gombrich notes that it was Alberti who first proposed the idea of viewing a painting as a window through which to look at the visible world. Leonardo da Vinci then gave substance to this idea by suggesting that "perspective is nothing else than seeing a place behind a pane of glass, quite transparent, on the surface of which the objects behind the glass are to be drawn" (299). Magritte plays with and subverts both of these ideas in *Evening Falls* (fig. 18) and in the 1949 version of *The Domain of Arnheim*. The landscape is visible on the pane of glass inside the room and in the distance through the aperture of the broken window. Fragments of the glass and the landscape lean against the wall and the window sill. The painting is, in fact, an "impossible" rendition of transparency and perspective. It violates our senses while parodying the idea of painting as a window on the world. Magritte has indeed broken with reality and realism. He himself acknowledges that the problem of the window led to the painting of *The Human Condition I* (fig. 15), one of the variations of *The Beautiful Captive* (plate 27).

> I placed in front of a window, seen from inside a room, a painting representing exactly that part of the landscape that was hidden from view by the painting. Therefore, the tree represented in the painting hid from view the tree situated behind it, outside the room. It existed for the spectator simultaneously inside the room on the painting and in his mind outside on the real landscape. This is how we see the world. We see it as outside us even though the representation of it is within us.
>
> (*EC* 144)

Magritte's intention in this painting, as José Vovelle points out, is to multiply the ambiguities and contradictions (130). The inside and the outside are joined deliberately. Either the canvas is transparent or the window is opaque. Like *The Beautiful Captive*, this painting raises fundamental questions concerning the ambiguity of perception, the structure of reality, and the phenomenology of the self.

Magritte painted several versions of *The Human Condition*. One of these, *The Human Condition II* (plate 66), may be viewed as a nonidentical twin of *The Beautiful Captive* (1967 [plate 27]). The easel is different, but the overlapping of canvas and seascape is the same. The clouds are missing, but the sky is there, as are the sea, the waves, and the sand. The round object, as before, is to the left of the easel. Instead of curtains

---

5. See Ben Stoltzfus, *Alain Robbe-Grillet*. Patrick Waldberg believes that *The Beautiful Captive* initiates a critical diptych that addresses reality and its representation; see his *René Magritte*, 181.

there are a wall and an arched doorway. The one striking difference between *The Beautiful Captive* series and *The Human Condition* series, be they seascapes or landscapes, is that the "captives" are always outside, whereas the "humans" are always inside and outside, simultaneously. *The Human Condition* inevitably structures a dialectic between the room, that is, the inside, and the landscape beyond the window. In the *Beautiful Captive* series the landscape outside never comes indoors; "beautiful captives" are never viewed from inside a room. Nevertheless, the ambiguity of perception in all these paintings suggests that the confrontation between real space and spatial illusion is irreconcilable.

It seems clear that *The Beautiful Captive*, in her many metamorphoses, is as central to Magritte's work as she is to Robbe-Grillet's. She is *The Central Story* (plate 37). This painting depicts the suitcase represented on the cover of the novel of the French edition; the painting also depicts a tuba, like the burning tuba in the 1947 version of *The Beautiful Captive* (fig. 1), and a woman with a cloth over her head and neck, her left hand on her throat. The cloth covering the head and the gesture of strangulation remind us so forcefully of Magritte's drowned mother that it is difficult to disassociate that tragic event from his art. Vanessa, the drowned virgin of Robbe-Grillet's novel—the suitcase also connotes virginity (since it is one of the props in *The Virgin's Chariot* [plate 71])—figures as an element in the text's "main story line." Finally, the word *tuba*, in French, may be written *tue bas*—"kill low"—which reinforces through paronomasia the connotation of death by drowning. Sometimes the French word *bombardon* is used to signify "tuba," but it does not lend itself to this kind of ambiguity. Moreover, a tuba exists in order to be played, and the word "play," connoting both games and the theater, describes the aesthetic of both Magritte and Robbe-Grillet. They play with reality, and they dramatize the language of art. Reality is also a mystery, and it is the mystery of life that Magritte alludes to over and over in his *Écrits complets*. He speaks of objects hiding other objects in the belief that there is always something hidden behind the face of reality. As we have seen, reflexive language veils, but it also unveils. To dramatize this idea, Magritte paints apples in front of men's faces: in *The Great War* (plate 59) and *The Son of Man*, a green apple hides a portion of a man's face. Inasmuch as there is also something hidden behind curtains, art for Magritte is an unveiling of affinities and relationships that usually remain obscured.

The affinities and relationships may be formulated as follows: *The Traveler* (fig. 19) on life's stage journeys between birth and death. His or her accouterments are a suitcase for the voyage and a tuba, since life, in one way or another, has to be played. Moreover, every person is the captive of a biological time span that pushes him or her toward death—hence the anonymity of the woman wearing the cloth covering on her head. *The Central Story* (plate 37) of life is thus always triple: the voyage, the game, the captive. Life is an enigma wrapped in a mystery. Whose face is behind the cloth covering? What is in the suitcase and why is it closed? Robbe-Grillet reinforces the mystery by telling us that the attaché case contains a wind instrument, or that it is the doctor's bag containing syringes, or that it is the murderer's attaché case.

Robbe-Grillet's and Magritte's predilection for murder mysteries gives an ironic touch to the existential anguish lurking behind the scenes. Since veiled, masked, and hidden faces play an important role in police stories and detective thrillers, both artists incorporate them into their work. In addition to his Fantômas paintings (e.g., *The Backfire*), Magritte wrote articles on Fantômas, Nick Carter, and Nat Pinkerton. *The Glass Key* is a Magritte painting and the title of one of Dashiell Hammett's novels.

Insofar as *The Murderer Threatened* (plate 4) connotes a detective story, it is a "key" painting for Magritte and Robbe-Grillet, whose novels so frequently have a whodunit flavor. Much of *La Belle Captive*'s diegesis, as we shall see, derives from this painting, which contains many of Magritte's and Robbe-Grillet's code images: the captive, the suitcase, the bowler-hatted men, and the parallel lines of the floor streaking toward the open window. The naked victim lying on the sofa, like the stone in *The Castle of the Pyrenees*, is an evocative image, one that carries Robbe-Grillet's plot, in its narrative as well as its clandestine sense, "toward pleasure." *Toward Pleasure* (plate 69), the painting, further dramatizes the connection between art and captive, usually a virgin.

Magritte and Robbe-Grillet, although referring to the painterly and the writerly processes, deliberately invoke or evoke images that produce ambiguity and tension between the objective world, the subjective imagination, and the means used to represent these seemingly different levels of reality.

THE VIRGIN'S CHARIOT

If we refer again to the suitcase on the French novel's cover and to *The Virgin's Chariot* (plate 71), a painting that depicts the suitcase on the reflecting surface of the hand mirror, we note that the mirror seems to be "transporting" the suitcase as the carriage, if there were one, might transport a virgin. However, the mirror is more an imaginary conveyance than a real one, and the suggested voyage is surely fictional rather than actual. And since the mirror does not appear on the novel's cover, the text will be *The False Mirror* (plate 31), that is, the eye/I of the writer and the reader that will reflect a fictional "order" in Magritte's paintings.

A suitcase may signify many things: traveling, intrigue (the center of a whodunit), self-enclosure (or the complacency of ownership), property, or business (perhaps it is *Le Voyeur*'s suitcase). It is primarily an image of containment, showing its outside and hiding its contents while asserting that it exists. A suitcase, like the novel, may be opened and its contents inspected. However, Magritte's association of the suitcase in the painting with the word "virgin" in the title coincides so neatly with Robbe-Grillet's own writerly intentions that it belies the suitcase's practical functions. Insofar as Robbe-Grillet gives his novel a corporeality that also downgrades its utilitarian function, the reader of necessity comes to view the beautiful captive as a metaphor for the body of the text. Moreover, since virginity, immolation, and sacrifice are mythic elements woven into the novel's structural patterns, the reader is encouraged to open the book as she or he would open a suitcase. Implicit in this metaphorical opening is the implied defloration of the virgin. The mythic levels within Robbe-Grillet's text authorize such liberties.

If the suitcase signifies "virgin," then the "beautiful captive" of the title is endowed with a virginity that Robbe-Grillet exploits in the text. The closed suitcase—like the book that is still virginal, unread, and unopened (reminiscent of Mallarmé's obsession with the white page)—is the metaphor of an artistic process that substitutes a woman for the body of the text and in which reading and writing are a form of penetration leading to a defloration. "It would be idle to dwell on the story of the ship, . . . or on the so-called rape (or on the metaphorical image of the bleeding flower)" (above, 30).

Robbe-Grillet is quite explicit on these matters and has—in an essay that is also a film project, "Fur Trap" ("Piège à fourrure")—described the nine stages of the metaphorical rape he is pursuing. Part 1 of *La Belle Captive* incorporates these nine stages, beginning with the falling stone (*The Castle of the Pyrenees*) and ending with the figurative text. Since we are dealing with an assault on language as well as with the ritualized stages of a conventional thriller, Robbe-Grillet simultaneously incorporates and devalues the coded stereotypes of the murderer, his footsteps, the knife, the cry, the wound, blood, the open door or window, the rape, the falling body: "Suddenly, ripping the silence apart, the cry of a woman is heard" (above, 15). These nine categories of part 1 form a network of coded messages that is one of the strands of his textual weave. However, the messages remain subordinate to the overriding artistic process that is described alternately as a game and as a theatrical experience. *The Idol*, the title of Magritte's stone bird flying over the seascape (plate 13), is being performed at the Opera even as the narrator abducts his unconscious victim and places her on a gaming table, defenseless, ready for the evening's pleasurable immolation (37).

Fertilization is perhaps one of the corollaries of defloration. It is indeed a fertile text that transforms stones into eggs, birds, idols, and so on. The text, like a fertilized ovum, is self-generating. However, since every reader approaches the text anew, its virginity must be self-restoring, and the text, like any good phoenix, is in the process of renewing itself. The narrative's pursuit of pleasure is also an invitation to reread, since the circular, open-ended nature of all New Novels requires rereading for maximal penetration.

Whenever Magritte and Robbe-Grillet go out "in search of pleasure," we may be sure that a latent eroticism will soon focus on a woman's body. Pleasure, as Roland Barthes suggests in *The Pleasure of the Text* (67), may culminate in a formalist orgasm, but with Magritte and Robbe-Grillet it is likely to be an exploration and/or parody of a mythic image or cultural leitmotif. *The Fanatics* (plate 16) depicts the birth (or is it the demise?) of the Phoenix hovering over the flames that will consume it and from which it will be reborn. *The Invention of Fire* (plate 65)—Magritte alludes to pleasure and to the fire that results from the rubbing together of two bodies—depicts a baluster between the spread legs of a naked woman. As for Robbe-Grillet, his apparent fascination with rape, torture, and deflowered virgins seems to stem, at least in part, from his desire to expose the inflated imagery of contemporary eroticism. In "Sur le choix des générateurs," he says:

> My generative themes are chosen more and more . . . from our contemporary popular imagery ("popular" in the widest sense, since these images in our so-called advanced societies circulate freely from one class to another): the illustrated covers of novels sold in stations, giant posters, the pornographic pulps of sex shops, the slick publicity of fashion magazines.
>
> (161)

Magritte's art, like Robbe-Grillet's, is full of references to popular and mythic images: mermaids, Fantômas, and even schoolbooks, as in *The Interpretation of Dreams* (fig. 6), a painting that associates words and images. *Collective Invention* (plate 48) is an inverted mermaid. *The Backfire* (plate 75) depicts Fantômas holding a rose in his hand instead of a dagger. In *The Interpretation of Dreams* the word *sky* is used to signify a suitcase. In each case the conventional meaning of a word is altered or perverted because, says Magritte: "As long as we surrealists have the means to act, we will not fail to oppose the myths, the ideas, the feelings and behavior of this equivocal world" (*EC* 135).

Magritte's painting *The Rape* (fig. 17) not only mirrors these intentions but also distills the expression "sex on the mind" to its quintessential form. Magritte substitutes a woman's breasts for her eyes, her navel for a nose, and her pubis for a mouth. Her hair frames the contours of a female body that has now become a head. This "rape of commonsense . . . in broad daylight," as James T. Soby phrases it (15), is like Robbe-Grillet's "fur trap," whose purpose is to parody the conventions of eroticism, horror, and the detective novel.

Borges has argued that all the great books since the end of the nineteenth century have been detective stories: *The Trial, The Turn of the Screw, Sanctuary.* Robbe-Grillet echoes and paraphrases Borges in the essay "Le Sadisme contre la peur" (48). Robbe-Grillet's parody of the detective novel thus moves beyond the realm of the thriller to include the so-called classical texts, as does Magritte's, whose titles are borrowed from the works of Poe, Baudelaire, Laclos, Breton, and others. Indeed, the pseudoplot of *La Belle Captive* revolves around abduction and murder. The painting *The Murderer Threatened* sets the stage, so to speak, for a series of events that culminate in the "murderer's" return to the scene of the "crime" in order to retrieve the doctor's bag—the incriminating evidence. The different themes of the novel repeat themselves, overlap, and bifurcate as the murder mystery theme is woven into the fabric of the text. The novel's themes (the murder mystery is one of them) become the basic elements engendering its architecture. In his essay "Après *l'Eden et après*," Robbe-Grillet says: "Far from disappearing, the anecdote thus begins to multiply; discontinuous, plural, mobile, uncertain, designating its own fictive nature, it becomes a 'game' in the strongest sense of the term" (48).

It would seem that the mirror in *The Virgin's Chariot* has transported us some distance from the initial juxtaposition with the suitcase. This is precisely the intent of surrealism's odd couplings and "fortuitous encounters." The suitcase, like Lautréamont's dissecting table, holds more than meets the eye, since the defloration of the virgin, like the falling stone, is one of the forces that keeps the novel in motion. However, we must never forget that the "violation" of the fair captive is a metaphor for the artistic process, for the writer struggling to overcome the conventions of stereotype and language.

Conventional novels move toward climax the way intercourse strives for orgasm. *La Belle Captive*, like Barthes's *Plaisir du texte*, also has pleasure in mind, accentuating the play, the texture of words, the detours, the fantasy, the in-and-out imagery, the very sexuality of the text. Claude Simon's *Corps conducteurs* is an apt title for similar body-texts, like Pinget's *Passacaille*, Ricardou's *Prise de Constantinople*, or Robbe-Grillet's *Souvenirs du triangle d'or*. Language in these novels and in others like them is treated as a body—a body of words whose corporeality and resourcefulness are a source of pleasure and delight. Textuality and sexuality are one. This erotic interweaving of Robbe-Grillet's imagery has its origins in the Latin term *texere*, "to weave." Moreover, as Mary Daly points out in *Gyn/Ecology: The Metaethics of Radical Feminism* (4–5), *texere* "is the origin and root both for *textile* and for *text*." Daly stresses the irony in the split of the word's meaning: for women the process of cosmic weaving has been kept at the level of the manufacture and maintenance of textiles, whereas " 'texts' are the kingdom of males." It is precisely this stereotype that Robbe-Grillet pursues within the body of *La Belle Captive*—a quest that uses the suitcase as a metaphorical image for the text and for the virgin.

The suitcase that figures so prominently in Magritte's pictures is described in the text as a small leather case belonging to a false doctor (142). The narrator—who should know better because he is simultaneously narrator, prisoner, student, and false doctor—speculates concerning its contents. He wonders if it might not be a musician's case containing a wind instrument (148)—perhaps a tuba, since the painting *Threatening Weather* (plate 73) depicts a woman's torso, a tuba, and a chair suspended in the sky. The narrator appropriates the wooden chair with the cane seat and sits down in the corridor in order to reflect on the strange situation in which he finds himself; he then notices blood flowing from under the closed door. The reader need not open it to know that a captive has either been deflowered, if she is a virgin, or if not, is being tortured in one of several ritual scenes at the Night Palace, where, in a performance entitled *The Beautiful Captive*, women submit to the "rosy crucifixion" or the "baluster"—*more canino*. Robbe-Grillet, with Marcel Duchamp in mind, describes both scenes as "la mariée mise à nue sur une machine." Magritte's *Invention of Fire* (plate 65) nicely illustrates the proposed ordeal and Robbe-Grillet's comic touch.

The doctor's attaché case is also the narrator's bag of tricks containing a variety of syringes, drugs, narcotics, and who knows what else (not chloroformed sandwiches, says a wry voice), hat pins perhaps, since the "doctor" deliberately inserts the syringe in the areola of the student's right breast in order to find out if she is conscious: "I insert the *needle* [my emphasis] with calculated slowness, rotating it like a gimlet. . . . I observe carefully the sweet face of my victim" (94–97). But the narrator is running out of time and cannot force his patient to submit to new "sensitivity tests" (98). These sensitivity controls seem more like an intertextual reference to Michelet's *Sorcière* than to useful medical or literary practice. Indeed, in the sixteenth and seventeenth centuries in France hat pins were inserted into the fleshy zones of alleged sorceresses in order to prove or disprove their possession by demons, a point that underscores and complicates the novel's imagery and vocabulary. The text also refers us to photographs depicting stereotyped dungeon scenes of torture: "the photograph on the red-and-black prayer stool, hands bound with a rosary, *the hat pins* [my emphasis], and so forth. Old phantoms . . . Old phantoms . . ." (134).

Considering Magritte's and Robbe-Grillet's treatment of women, some readers may be tempted to think of the two artists as sadists. To view their works as sexist, however, is to minimize the energy and the liberating roles they both attribute to women. The surrealists believed that it was Woman who would redeem the world. As for the sadoerotic elements in Robbe-Grillet's works, it would be a mistake to interpret them as unconscious fixations; rather, they represent his parodic treatment of our collective unconscious, his exaggeration of the violence, eroticism, and death that are the hallmark of the twentieth century.

In line with the novel's spirit of wry humor, if not "black magic," I am tempted to refer to the attaché case as *Pandora's Box* (plate 18). Indeed, if we pursue all the appropriate metaphorical slippages and analogies, it is a can of fish (if not worms) containing dismembered mermaids (the emblem on the tuna cans labeled "Chicken of the Sea" is a mermaid), forbidden worlds (see Magritte's painting *The Forbidden Universe*, which depicts a reclining mermaid on a love seat [plate 62]), mythical practices, abducted goddesses, and deflowered virgins.

Robbe-Grillet has filled the doctor's case with objects worthy of Fantômas and imbued Magritte's *Virgin's Chariot* with meaningful juxtapositions reminiscent of Lautréamont's dissecting table. A Fantômas bouquet, like the chloroformed sandwich, exudes a lethal fragrance. Fantômas's chair, like Robbe-Grillet's booby-trapped eggs that give birth to David and Vanessa, explodes; a wet rope is a snake, a cupboard is a hallway, doors provide "unexpected" openings, if not "answers," and windows, when not false, open "in praise of the dialectic." These incessant disruptions of reality have their desired effect of estrangement.

In Robbe-Grillet's text an abandoned factory, fish, mermaids, and girls are "literally" dissected before being canned, assembled, labeled with the familiar mermaid sticker, and shipped. Certain objects, such as the "phallomorphic" baluster, the woman's shoe, and the sacrificial table, further reinforce the Lautréamont connection. The baluster was used to deflower Vanessa. The shoe is a highly charged "sacred object"—all that is left of the drowned virgin. It bursts into flame, connoting both woman and sexuality. The sacrificial table is there for the immolation of minor goddesses. The appropriate Magritte illustrations are *The Difficult Crossing* (plates 8 and 33), and *The Depths of Pleasure* (plate 30), all of which incorporate the baluster; *God Is Not a Saint* (plate 51), which depicts the shoe; and *The Murderer Threatened* (plate 4) and *The Visible World* (plate 20), which depict the sacrificial bed and table. As a juxtaposed triad, the baluster, the shoe, and the bed are "aflame" with mythic sexuality (*The Fanatics* [plate 16] shows a phoenix hovering over a fire). There is more: the narrator's black Cadillac is referred to as an "ambulance-hearse," the false student is "fair game," and the scalpel used to cut away her dress in order to reveal the "sacred triangle" is necrological and phallic. The narrator has the imagination of a necrophiliac. All of these objects are woven into the text as he opens door after door at the canning factory in pursuit of the meaning of Magritte's titles and the labyrinth of words that contains them. Finally, the adjective "beautiful" in the novel's title echoes Lautréamont's famous dictum concerning the *beauty* of such juxtapositions: they may shock our sensibilities, as indeed the surrealists wanted them to, but the Freudian undercurrent of sexuality that propels *The Virgin's Chariot* gives these highly charged sequences an affective thrust and artistic validity that is undeniable.[6]

LABYRINTHS, LANGUAGE, AND CELLS

The labyrinths of our unconscious mind, of myth, and of historical practice, combining eroticism and violence, are the leitmotifs of Robbe-Grillet's antinovels. The labyrinth motif is, in fact, omnipresent. The world of objects is treated as a maze, and language proliferates into a labyrinth of associations. We should perhaps note that in *Course in General Linguistics* Saussure compares the word to "a house in which the arrangement and function of different rooms has been changed several times" (183). If each word is like a mansion with many rooms, then language is indeed a labyrinth of many corridors. As Magritte and Robbe-Grillet wander through this ambiguous but signifying system, they open one door after another, describe the contents of one room after another, escape, are imprisoned, and escape again, wrestling all the while with words, objects, images, myth, and the unconscious. In *The Tomb of the Wrestlers* (plate 7), the room—even as it illustrates the confinement of the "captive" rose—aptly describes the struggle between the artist's *parole* and society's *langue*. Each word, each sentence,

6.   For additional information on the Lautréamont connection, see Claudette Oriol-Boyer, "Les Cicatrices de la mémoire"; see also Raillard, "Mots de passe," 208.

and each paragraph of the novel together form a labyrinth of associations, as one image slips into another, as associations intertwine, as the motifs multiply.

In this context *La Belle Captive* describes the abandoned canning factory, the Night Palace, and the Opera as a physical maze "whose imposing or secret doors succeed each other in identical series from one end to the other of the semicircular corridors, as well as the long straight hallways that crisscross the upper floors, not to mention the labyrinths occupying the various basements" (131). The narrator opens the doors to secret rooms that contain the "sacred objects" of Magritte's art (and Robbe-Grillet's)—objects that are used by Robbe-Grillet in order to generate new fictional episodes. Each of these rooms is a cell that is described in part or in whole. There is a progression from stone to egg to room to prison. All of these objects and places are linked to the cell as an enclosure, as a biological entity, as a reproductive force, and as a linguistic unit, be it a word or an image. The labyrinth is thus composed of cells or rooms containing different objects: the rose in *The Tomb of the Wrestlers* is one of these; *The Listening Room* (down the hall, no doubt) is another (plate 54). These paintings depict rooms filled by incongruously huge objects: a vast rose, and a giant apple as big as the enclosure.

The dramatization of the room as cell begins as soon as the falling rock outside moves inside to dwarf the two men standing in the arched opening (*Portrait of a Woman* [plate 2]). *The Invisible World* (plate 3), although retaining the vista of the sea and the sky—visible through the open door and the balcony—brings the rock inside the room. The two cells, the rock and the room, provide a metaphoric image of the creative process. The stone egg, and eventually the egg alone, will be the embryo from which the novel will emerge—the parthenogenetic egg that spawns David and Vanessa.

A cell is thus both the enclosure and the enclosed, both *langue* and *parole*, the inside and the outside. The cell is a metaphor for all language, since language envelops us, determines our perception of reality, precedes our birth, contains all values. I as a person am, among other things, a vehicle that transmits language from one generation to the next. I do not think language; language thinks through me. "JE est un autre" (I is another), as Rimbaud would say. Hence the doubling of narrative identities and the presence of twins or *sosies* who are there in order to dramatize the presence of the other, as in *Not to Be Reproduced* (plate 24): "These are no doubt my features. But my entire physiognomy seems to have lost all character, all identity; it is a standard head, an anonymous form; henceforth I resemble the robot-portrait of the murderer that appeared in the newspapers" (54). This anonymous "person," this language that we all speak, is a great transmitter of clichés, common values, and ready-made attitudes. Language as an anonymous force communicates bias, hate, prejudice, religious faith, mythic truths, patriotic fervor. The cohesion of social units, be they family, church, town, province, or nation, depends on the orchestration of value systems that are transmitted through organized linguistic codes: the flag, pictures, relics, statues, buildings, places—all the sacred cows of nationhood and religious obeisance. Schools, churches, books, radio, and television teach and communicate ideology. In the United States, for example, the alliance between Protestantism and capitalism has produced "the big money," as John Dos Passos calls it. The recognized ideology of the United States is that "business is its business." It is clear that all our industries have one objective: profit. This ideology may be viewed as a poisonous cloud enveloping our consciousness, contaminating everything.[7]

This seepage of ideology into language and the subconscious recalls Magritte's painting *Poison* (plate 72). It depicts an empty room, a partly opened door, the inevitable seascape visible through the open door, and a white cloud in the doorway. Ideology resembles this cloud. It invades. Frequently we are unaware of its presence since the language we learned as children contains within itself the values of the social unit we inhabit. Jacques Lacan insists that it is language that names objects and structures our reality. Language is that "other" who speaks as though from some unknown region of the unconscious. Like the cloud, language has seeped into my inner room. Says Magritte: "My art is valid only insofar as it opposes bourgeois ideology in whose name life is being extinguished" (*EC* 85).

Whether as a species or as individuals, says Barthes, humans do not exist prior to language ("To Write" 135). Language constructs the world about us. It is a tool that seems to come from within, because we use it (as I am using it now), but that always precedes our readiness to harness it. As Robbe-Grillet comments:

> To pick up on Saussure's famous opposition, I do not work on *langue*
> (this twentieth-century French that I use just as I have received it)
> but on society's *parole* (the discourse of the people with whom I live).
> Except that I, in turn, refuse to speak this particular *parole*; I use it as
> raw material, which means that I push it back to its role as *langue*,
> from which, finally, I develop my own discourse.
>
> ("Sur le choix des générateurs" 160)

Much of Robbe-Grillet's discourse consists in "playing" with *langue*, a form of play that constantly emphasizes its theatrical dimensions. Patrick Waldberg maintains that

---

7.   Another poisonous cloud, from Magritte's point of view, was the ideology of communism. In 1945 Magritte and Paul Nougé joined the Belgian Communist Party in order to help shape the Party's cultural and artistic goals from within. Magritte submitted several posters, but all were rejected. He explained: "We were dealing with people who were deaf. . . . Conformity here was as rampant as it was in the most conservative bourgeois circles. After several months I stopped going to the meetings and had no further contact with the party. There was no exclusion or break, but, as far as I was concerned, the disenchantment was total and the distancing final" (quoted in Waldberg, *René Magritte*, 210).

the curtains in Magritte's paintings are always there to remind us that "the mind is a theater directed by mystery" (21).

The words "play," "theater," "scene," "representation," "decor," and "opera" are also used in order to dramatize *parole* as a "presence," in order to incorporate it as a character-actor on the writerly stage that the novel constructs for us. The narrator says: "The final scene is identical, as well as the decor. . . . All I have to do in order to alert those who will carry her to the other side, toward the cruel fate reserved for young goddesses, is to tap a coded rhythm with the tip of my cane—three sharp raps" (122). In the French theater the three taps of the cane signal the opening of the curtains—the beginning of the play. In addition to being an actor, the narrator has now become a stage director. His *parole* is in dialogue with the *langue* of the bowler-hatted interrogators, who, out of the blue, ask him what he meant by the "seaweed" and the "shell." The dramatization is played out as the voice of the establishment tries to muzzle the voice of the artist. Is the narrator not in the cell, and are not the bowler-hatted men the guards? Gablik asserts that the collective physiognomy of the bowler-hatted man is representative of a group soul with a mythological aspect: "He has come to represent all men" (156).

The narrator answers, as though the question were both logical and pertinent, saying that the seaweed is a metaphor for the girl's long blonde hair, whereas the shell is nothing more than a kind of porcelain (122–24). But the description of the shell is so eroticized as to leave no doubt as to its metaphorical intent. Magritte's "familiar objects" (plate 61) now come into full focus as Robbe-Grillet toys with them, giving each one an erotic charge for the performance he is describing, that is, the artistic performance of "forbidden" myths whose *parole* is being censored by the *langue* of the bowler-hatted men. The narrator may be in a cell, but it is clear that *langue* is now *his* captive and that he is playing with its metaphorical and representational connotations. The narrator's *parole* is asserting "artistic license." Robbe-Grillet comments: "It's not a question of ridding myself once and for all of all the mythic elements that surround me, but, on the contrary, *to speak them*, i.e., to exercise the power of my freedom over them instead of being trapped by them" ("Sur le choix des générateurs" 161).

In spite of Robbe-Grillet's claim that his *parole* is free, the text's narrative voice retains a disturbing ambiguity that slips back and forth between Robbe-Grillet, the author (who may be exercising his freedom), and somebody else's imagination that projects erotic obsessions onto "innocent" objects like the seashell. Ultimately it may be the reader who falls for the metaphorical trap that Robbe-Grillet lays for him or her (see Magritte's *Familiar Objects*).

Meanwhile, the interrogators ask once more if there is a rapport between the "representation"—a word that connotes theater and painting—of the shell and the sponge, the lemon, the pitcher, and so on, the "familiar objects" of Magritte's painting. The answer is revealing and not unexpected:

An obvious connection! Of a sacrificial order. . . . The sponge soaked in acid is inserted into the opening of the shell . . . Surely you are familiar with the effect that lemon juice has when squeezed on the flesh of an oyster, and the way the delicate membraned fringes retract under the burning.

(124)

As though aroused by the shell's "erotic charge" and the word "burning," the interrogator asks about the "fire" at the Opera. The word "fire" then evokes the burning shoe as the carefully orchestrated slippage of associations, one after another, educes the adolescent idol, the sacrificial table, the phallic toy (the baluster), the cigar of the false voyeur (an allusion to Magritte's *State of Grace* [plate 36], which depicts a bicycle on a smoking cigar—an intertextual allusion to *Le Voyeur*), the candle, and the burning tampon (intertextual references to *Projet pour une révolution à New York* and *Souvenirs du triangle d'or*), and so on.

[*Interrogator:*]   Is the virginity of the subject indispensable?
    [*Narrator:*]   In theory, yes.

(124)

Virginity indeed! Robbe-Grillet's "representation" of the seashell, the sponge, and the lemon no longer corresponds to Magritte's rendition of these seemingly prosaic objects. The text's subjective slippage incorporates them into the novel's mythoerotic diegesis. Clearly Robbe-Grillet has exercised the same arbitrary nomenclature that Magritte has in *The Interpretation of Dreams* (fig. 6), in which a bag is called "the sky." Robbe-Grillet transforms seaweed into hair and a seashell into a vagina whose "virginity" is a "desirable" facet of the mythic ritual he alludes to. This is an imaginary although by no means trivial game that Robbe-Grillet is playing on all linguistic registers, and it dramatizes the two elements of the writerly process that are in perpetual conflict: *langue* and *parole*.

VICTORIOUS AND VANQUISHED

On the novel's immediate and superficial level, the "beautiful captive" is a young girl who is abducted, raped with a baluster (Magritte's *bilboquet*), and drowned—a reference, says the narrator, to the well-known episode of "the difficult crossing." *The Difficult Crossing* is the title of Magritte's painting depicting the picture (or is it perhaps a window?) of a storm-tossed ship being watched from inside a room by a baluster with a human eye (plate 8).[8] This initial treatment of the drowned Vanessa is in keeping with Robbe-Grillet's belief that woman plays a dual role in the public's mythic mind: on the one hand, she is the exalted religious figure of the Virgin; on the other, she is the debased figure of the victim:

> In the entrance to the hallway [of the temple of phantasms], on either side of the wide dual spiral staircase, stand the two monumental statues of the ancient divinity of pleasure in her double appearance: Victorious Vanadis and Vanquished Vanadis.
>
> (128)

The famous *Victory of Samothrace*, a statue of a woman, is in the Louvre. Delacroix's painting *Liberté guidant le peuple* depicts a woman "inspiring" the fighters at the barricades. As for woman as victim, Michelet (whose ideas have influenced Robbe-Grillet) has analyzed her historical presence with great acuity in *La Sorcière*. In *Essais critiques*, Barthes says that the element in woman that fascinates Michelet is not her nudity, which in itself is a banal theme, but what she is hiding. The element that gives woman a role comparable to the ocean's tides (also influenced by lunar cycles) is her sanguineous function: "The husband's right and joy, is in acceding to *nature's secret*, to possess finally in Woman, as a result of her incredible communion, a mediatrix between man and the Universe" (119).

Michelet's analyses are the source, in part, for Robbe-Grillet's "manhandling" of woman in *Glissements progressifs du plaisir* and in *La Belle Captive*.[9] Robbe-Grillet combines the two myths, thereby creating a victor-victim, a Marie-Eve (the heroine of *L'Eden et après*), whose name connotes a virgin and a sinner, a heroine who is always fresh, whole, and untouched no matter how many times she is violated. The names may change, but the woman remains the same, be she Marie-Ange, the heroine of the film *La Belle Captive*, or the novel's "beautiful captive," Anne-Marie in her cage, smiling enigmatically out of the night. Georges Raillard sees this Magritte picture as an inversion of Duchamp's "de la mariée à la vierge"—that is, Anne followed by Marie

8.   In discussing *The Difficult Crossing*, José Vovelle refers to De Chirico's influence on Magritte, particularly the statues, mannequins, and balusters that play such a frequent and prominent role in their paintings. Magritte calls De Chirico "the first painter to have thought of making painting speak of something other than painting" (*EC* 484). Vovelle believes that in Magritte's painting there is an ongoing and reversible process of humanization and dehumanization of objects and people: the baluster has a human eye even as the human body is reduced to stone (89, 123).

9.   See Michalczyk, "Robbe-Grillet, Michelet, and Barthes."

instead of vice versa (207). Genet incorporates woman's mythic duality into *Le Balcon*: Chantal, the martyr of the revolution, is a heroic whore. Robbe-Grillet has remarked in an interview in *Diacritics*:

> The stereotype of woman in our society is double; hence, it is also double in my books and films. The stereotype of woman is, on the one hand, the slavewoman, the woman made servile, tortured, dominated, and, on the other hand, the stereotype which is just as important in our whole culture is the symbol of freedom. Freedom, the image of freedom in all of painting, in all of literature, is always a woman.
>
> (Mistacco 43)

Some readers err in thinking that Robbe-Grillet endorses these stereotypes or that he derives pleasure from their alleged realism. The specular modes, reflexive elements, and intratextual allusions—all the devices that foreground language by calling attention to the process of writing rather than to the adventures in writing—deny mimesis and devalue nature. The New Novel, like a modern painting, wants first and foremost to be an object, to be a surface that sight responds to. In *Art and Illusion* E. H. Gombrich quotes a woman visiting Matisse's studio who once said: "But surely, the arm of this woman is much too long." The artist replied: "Madame, you are mistaken. This is not a woman, this is a picture" (115).

In the film *Glissements progressifs du plaisir*, it is Alice who seduces the magistrate, the lawyer, and the priest, that is, the "law and order" representatives of the male establishment. Alice stabs Nora, the whore, with a pair of scissors, an act of violence directed against servility, but before "stabbing" her, she plays with Nora's body—the body of language; the *langue* that Robbe-Grillet is manipulating—by painting her body. The film incorporates violence as a metaphor of subversion.

This subversion functions simultaneously on two levels. The first, which is linguistic, takes its cues from James Joyce, Raymond Roussel, and the Russian formalists, who maintain that reflexive art always draws our attention to its own internal self-regulating machinery. The second level of subversion depends on cultural stereotypes that are inflated and then parodied. Robbe-Grillet foregrounds units of establishment ideology and subverts them through reversal, exaggeration, and distortion. He plays with cultural myths, striving for a reversal that will affect the viewer's perspectives within a single pictorial world. His images violate normative codes even as diegesis turns plausibility and verisimilitude upside down. In *The Fantastic in Literature*, Eric Rabkin describes this reversal as the quality that defines fantasy as a genre (189, 217). Rabkin points out that George MacDonald stood theology on its head, that Lewis Carroll reversed the fundamental scientific tenets of his day, poking fun at history and religion, and that William Morris mocked religion and science. The fantastic, as practiced by these three writers, according to Rabkin, is important because it depends entirely on reality for its existence (28). Subversion is possible because reality is so securely fixed. Robbe-Grillet's ritual violence, like the Marquis de Sade's, uses the wrong side of things and the wrong side of words. And it is precisely because ideology is securely fixed that this reversal has meaning. To play with sex and violence is to subvert and at the same time to reinvent reality. Artists interested in fantasy and play derive their strength, their freedom, and their pleasure from such parodic acts.

Historically, in times of war the sacking of a besieged city has been accompanied by pillage and rape. On the mythic level, Jupiter raped Danae with a shower of gold. In literature, in William Faulkner's *Sanctuary* Popeye rapes Temple with a corncob. Robbe-Grillet foregrounds this tradition of sexual violence, incorporating it on the writerly level as the writer's assault on language, its conventions, and its clichés. The body of language (*langue*) is transformed into the body of the text (*parole*). In *La Belle Captive*, *langue* (the voice of the establishment) interrogates *parole* (the artist's voice) as the narrative mode alternates between male abductor and female victim, between interrogators dressed in black coats and bowler hats and the answers of the prisoner.

If language determines our perception of reality, how can the artist, while using language, create fresh and original views of the world—views that are not already conditioned? In short, how can a captive woman become a metaphor for language?

When language is foregrounded and when fiction becomes conscious of its own creative processes—that is, when it becomes reflexive—it develops characteristics that tend to downgrade the traditional roles of character, conflict, psychology, story, and denouement. The generative themes, the proliferation of stories, the textual polysemy, and paronomasia give the author leeway to exaggerate and subvert the coded conventions that fiction normally uses. The writer no longer tells stories; rather, he or she explores the story of telling.

This is the context in which Robbe-Grillet develops the notions of freedom and bondage, inside and outside, victim and murderer. He structures a dialectic of opposites, a dialogue of contradictions that are nevertheless profoundly related. If the *langue* of bourgeois interrogators imprisons, then the artist's *parole* liberates. In "Le Sadisme contre la peur" Robbe-Grillet says:

> It is not a question of closing my eyes to sex and violence, nor of condemning them, but of organizing them within a living *parole*. . . . What's needed . . . is not to speak about these matters, but to *voice them*, i.e., to invent a discourse that will control the pulsive forces, the images . . . of violence that, without our knowing it, threaten to overwhelm us. It is the organization of these images that structures the space within which my freedom asserts itself.

(48)

To voice these stereotypes in fictional or artistic form is to provide an outlet from the cultural prisons that govern our modes of thinking. To loosen the grip of social taboos on our daily lives is to provide alternative, perhaps freer, ways of thinking. The gap in which free thought and behavior begin to manifest themselves depends on bringing into consciousness the imagery of our subconscious, where fantasies have been accumulating stereotypes of fear, sex, and violence. Robbe-Grillet believes that the dramatization of this repressed material is a form of catharsis—a purgation that will perhaps reverse the sexist attitudes of Western ideology. In "Le Sadisme contre la peur" he says:

> Reading is a "catharsis," the spectacle a purgation. Those moralists who wish to interdict the showing of sex and blood are the ones we find behind the most repressive societies: Nazism was Puritan, Hitler chided Goebbels for his mistresses, persecuted homosexuals, burned the books he deemed immoral.

(48)

THE DEVIL'S SMILE

The relationship between the guard and his prisoner is one possible organization of those pulsive forces that illustrates the artist's independence from them. One cannot function without the other. This rapport may be compared to the relationship between a key and its keyhole. The keyhole exists for the key and vice versa. Without his prisoner a guard is superfluous; without a guard the prisoner is free. Without a doctor there is no patient. Where would sanity be if there were no madness, and so forth? It is this dialectic of necessary, inevitable, yet contrasting relationships that Robbe-Grillet and Magritte explore. In *The Devil's Smile* (plate 11) a small key "in profile" is seen in its entirety inside the keyhole. This exaggeration of the expected creates a shock of recognition. The "hot" supercharged key unlocks the door to understanding. "I then notice the small, shiny key in the keyhole. Strangely enough, it is hot to the touch, although this does not interfere with the proper functioning of the lock, quite to the contrary, perhaps, aha!" (32).

The narrator's exclamations, asides, and elliptical allusions seem to be in touch with a figurative undercurrent of meaning that is highlighted by Magritte's pictures. If one of my roles as reader, as it was originally for the writer, is not only to read the text and look at the pictures but to fill the gap between the two with meaning—that is, to produce a plausible fiction that will relate them—then the key is to the keyhole as the text is to the pictures. They function best together or in opposition; each one, in one way or another, engages the mechanism of the other. The hot key evokes a source of heat—fire—and indeed the painting *The Ladder of Fire* (plate 15) depicts a burning key. We already know that friction, fire, pleasure, and sexuality are related. This theme, as we shall see, is developed even further. Meanwhile, the key-keyhole title, *The Devil's Smile*, opens the door to additional speculation concerning connections with Michelet's *Sorcière*.

Robbe-Grillet's "false doctor," like the religious fanatics described by Michelet, probes for sensitive zones in the "false student's" body with needles that look like hat pins. If an alleged witch felt no pain after an insertion, she was accused of being possessed by the devil and burned at the stake. The description of such zeal and cruelty is enough to distress even the most callous reader. It's enough to drive one mad—or is madness on the side of the fanatics who perpetrate such outrageous practices? A judicious selection of Magritte's paintings from Robbe-Grillet's *Belle Captive* illustrates these historical practices: *The Ladder of Fire* is "the key" to understanding. *Black Magic* (plate 56) is the witches' brew. *The Fanatics* (plate 16), as a title, refers to the zealots, even as the fire in the picture burns the Phoenix, the bird that regenerates like sorceresses in France, who, from the twelfth century to the eighteenth, multiplied and flourished despite persecution. The "devil smiles" (32) with the complicity of male prosecutors.

If insight is one of "the keys" to pleasure, then this Freudian object is not without its erotic charge, as the reader and the narrator unlock one mysterious door after another in order to penetrate deeply into the virginal text. This may be the meaning Robbe-Grillet attributes to Magritte's painting *The Depths of Pleasure* (plate 30), a painting that depicts a naked woman with long flowing hair and closed eyes, holding on to her left breast with one hand and encircling a baluster that is as tall as she is with her right arm and hand. Flames lick the base of the baluster and the woman's hair. The titles of Magritte's paintings are as evocative as the images, and together they elicit metaphorical resonances that enrich the two. A picture entitled *The Empty Picture Frame* is a case in point: despite the title, the frame is not empty; rather, it depicts a wall of red bricks. What's more, Robbe-Grillet, like Magritte, exploits contradictions in order to dramatize the creative process with oxymorons that call attention to the text of *La Belle Captive*:

> There also remains the problem of the empty picture frame, which must have a direct link with the little key, a hidden rapport that would undoubtedly require a long explanation.
>
> (42)

The enigmatic empty frame that Robbe-Grillet refers to may belong to the 1947 version of Magritte's *The Beautiful Captive* (fig. 1)—a frame through which the seascape is visible—or it may refer to the painting entitled *The Empty Picture Frame*. In *René Magritte* Abraham Hammacher says that "the title remains a problem," a statement that duplicates Robbe-Grillet's words exactly (118). But what is the problem?

In the Marlborough Catalogue (1973), Emile Langui refers to this painting as *The Blood-letting*, dating it to around 1934. But Hammacher is unhappy with Langui's translation of the French *La Saignée*. In 1943 Marcel Mariën published the painting with the title *L'Oiseau qui n'a qu'une aile* (*The Bird with Only One Wing*). Hammacher keeps the title from the inventory of the Edward James Foundation, that is, *The Empty Picture Frame*; Sarah Whitfield, however, calls it *The Blood-letting* and dates it to around 1938 or 1939 (141). This painting, like the *Beautiful Captive* series, depicts a picture within a picture. The mystery derives from the fact that the bricks may be painted bricks, or they may belong to the wall behind the "empty frame" (provided, of course, that the paint and plaster have been removed), or they may be part of a wall on the other side of the street, in which case "the empty picture frame" is a window. Thus, Magritte has once again stressed painting as a false window on reality. Moreover, the falsehood has been compounded by the "problem" of the title, thereby giving us an ambiguity that enhances its appeal for Robbe-Grillet. Besides, in French a "saignée" also means a hole in the wall for repairs. No English word or title could possibly connote or denote the inherent ambiguity of the French.

Were it up to Robbe-Grillet to choose the title of the painting, he would surely have preferred the original French—*La Saignée*—with its connotations of blood, victim, and captive—connotations reinforced by the picture's thematic similarity with *The Beautiful Captive*. Besides, Robbe-Grillet, like Michelet, is interested in blood in general and in woman's sanguineous functions in particular—functions that stress her affinity with nature, lunar cycles, and rhythmic tides. Such an interest would have attracted him to *La Saignée* and probably explains the obscure allusion in his text to "the empty frame." An empty frame also reinforces the concept of absence and abduction, discussed above, in relation to *The Central Story* (plate 37), *The False Mirror* (plate 31), and *The Beautiful Captive* (plate 27).

Robbe-Grillet's and Michelet's fascination with blood in relation to woman as a mediatrix between man and nature is echoed, moreover, in other Magritte paintings, one of which, *The Blood of the World* (*Le Sang du monde*), shows organisms resembling legs and arms. The skin has been removed, revealing a circulatory system in red and black. There are also round forms in gray that resemble phases of rock formations (these also have red-and-black veins); in the background stand flesh-toned hills resembling Swiss cheese with red holes. The "sky" is black. Says Hammacher: "In *The World's Blood* one can discern the demon in Magritte's imagination, the obsession with a dark fertility urge which has a perverse side to it" (76). Magritte, Robbe-Grillet, and Michelet all seem to have a common interest in the world's "blood rhythms."

The two paintings *La Saignée* and *Le Sang du monde* are thus related not only by their titles but also by their inherent pictorial functions. To reveal the red-and-black circulatory system of the body by removing the skin is analogous to revealing the red bricks in the wall by removing the paint and plaster. The veil has been lifted and the picture speaks. We see what has been hidden or obscured—one of Magritte's most persistent themes.

Finally, the "explanation" for "the empty frame" that Robbe-Grillet refers to but does not provide is perhaps contained in this essay—an essay that will, I hope, unlock the door to that "remote room" wherein the fair captive, like the Mona Lisa, continues to smile enigmatically.

DIALECTICS, ARTIFICE, AND PIPES

After exploiting the surrealist aesthetic of distant and seemingly unrelated juxtapositions, Magritte explored contradictions of similarity. Instead of a bird in a cage, he painted an egg in a cage. Instead of a tree bearing a leaf, he painted a leaf that is a tree. Instead of a shoe containing a foot, he painted a foot becoming a shoe (*The Red Model*). Instead of an empty nightgown, he painted a "body-nightgown" fleshed out with breasts (*Philosophy in the Boudoir* [plate 29]). At the other end of the spectrum, *Hegel's Holiday* (plate 34) depicts an open umbrella holding a glass of water. An object designed to repel water is juxtaposed with an object designed to contain liquids. To shed and to hold—the joining of contrasting functions—is the inspiration of this witty and insightful painting.

In Praise of the Dialectic (plate 19) juxtaposes elements that are both similar and distant. It is a study in contradiction, a picture of the impossible, depicting an open window as viewed from outside a building. However, instead of seeing objects in a room, we see another building as though we were looking out from the inside. The room contains the building as the keyhole contains the key. It is impossible, but there is a logic of similitude. The narrator says: "Here I am . . . in front of my own open window. . . . A big mirror that occupies all of the visible wall behind the table (always the same one) reflects the bluish image of the house opposite, as though the outside of the room were on the inside" (44). Robbe-Grillet's text contradicts Magritte in the same way that Magritte contradicts reality. Magritte's painting has no mirror or table. The mirror is Robbe-Grillet's code image for the reflexive text, and the table is the code image for the writer at work.

If Magritte and Robbe-Grillet have a predilection for doors, windows, and mirrors, it is because these objects mark the interface between indoors and outdoors. Both artists break windows (see Magritte's *Evening Falls* [fig. 18] and *The Domain of Arnheim* [plate 10]) in order to emphasize the overlapping of perception between the inside and the outside. *The Unexpected Answer* (plate 23), showing a door with a hole in it—a hole that is vaguely representational of a human figure—suggests a startlingly easy passage from inside to outside. Such double images synthesize time and place. Events normally experienced separately coincide just as things are perceived simultaneously both inside and outside the mind. To confront the problem of language is to confront the problem of perception is to confront the problem of consciousness. These are ontological and epistemological problems that Wittgenstein, Magritte, and Robbe-Grillet address. Magritte and Robbe-Grillet have given artistic answers to philosophical, linguistic, and perceptual dilemmas.

The novel's narrative displacements, like Magritte's simultaneous contradictory paintings, occur without apparent logic or coherence. A narrator not only changes identities from one paragraph to the next but changes places within a paragraph or a sentence: from a beachside café to a prison cell; from a prison cell to the partially destroyed buildings of a seaside town; back and forth between prison and beach, between reality and fantasy—a reality that is fantasy, and a fantasy that is reality, that is, the reality of the text, a text that is undeniably present, artificial, antinatural, and unnatural.

This artificial reality engendered by the text uses the same everyday language with which all speakers and readers of French are familiar. Yet Robbe-Grillet, like Magritte, deals with one of the central issues of twentieth-century art: the collapse of the conventional devices of illusionistic representation. Magritte's painting of a pipe, entitled *The Treachery of Images* (fig. 14), incorporates the caption "This is not a pipe." Indeed, the painting of a pipe is not a pipe. The painting of a pipe is exactly what it is, the painting of a pipe. The pipe is something else, an object that one smokes. Says Magritte: "Who would dare pretend that the REPRESENTATION of a pipe IS a pipe? Who could smoke the pipe in my picture? Nobody. Therefore it IS NOT A PIPE" (*EC* 250). Magritte, always an ardent reader of philosophy, was an admirer of Foucault's work, and Foucault, the philosopher, literary critic, and art critic, reciprocated by writing a book about this painting entitled *Ceci n'est pas une pipe* (*This Is Not a Pipe*).

In a variant of this painting entitled *The Philosopher's Lamp*, Magritte emphasizes the point by inserting a man's nose into the bowl of a pipe, thereby negating the pipe's primary function as an object that can be smoked. The pipe is now a noseholder, similar in function to the candlestick next to it. But the caption, if there were one, could never say: "This is a noseholder." It would have to say: "This is not a noseholder." These two paintings, like the variations on *The Human Condition*, highlight the problem of language as a representational system. The word "pipe" is not the object "pipe." The signifier is not the signified. In *This Is Not a Pipe* Magritte demonstrates that an image is not the object it is meant to represent.

All of Wittgenstein's philosophy was a battle against the bewitchment of our intelligence by means of language, even as Saussure's *Course in General Linguistics* emphasized the arbitrary nature of signifiers. Magritte's painting *The Interpretation of Dreams* (fig. 6), while demystifying language, illustrates both of these tenets: the painting is divided into four panels depicting four objects with the names of these objects written underneath. But there is a glaring discrepancy: the signifier does not correspond to the signified. The bag is labeled "the sky"; the knife is labeled "the bird"; the leaf is called "the table"; and the sponge is called "a sponge." Magritte's paintings are all part of a contemporary crisis of language and consciousness: how do we cope with the gap between a representational system and the reality it purports to describe? Magritte's art raises fundamental questions concerning the nature and the origin of the system used. The series of paintings entitled *The Beautiful Captive* (plate 27), *The Human Condition I* (fig. 15), *The Interpretation of Dreams* (fig. 6), and *Familiar Objects* (plate 61) reveal the profound ambiguity and arbitrariness of any representational system, be it linguistic or pictorial.

CONSUMED MYTHS AND FLAMING FICTION

The evocative power of Magritte's images has contributed to a recent cultural phenomenon. Postcards of his paintings are sold in Europe, everywhere. *Collective Invention* (plate 48), depicting a mermaid with the head of a fish and the legs of a woman, also seems to have particular mythic appeal to the residents and tourists of Moslem countries around the Persian Gulf, where, according to Fernand Braudel, postcards of the mermaid, with captions in Arabic and French, read: "A real Siren found on the western shores of the Persian Gulf, 7/4/73" (53). This "plagiarism" reveals the living presence of one of the Mediterranean's oldest myths—the female archetype. As siren or idol, she incarnates the notion of the sacred throughout the Mediterranean basin.

Except for the element of fantasy, there is no ambiguity in the "representation" of a mermaid—that mythical creature that is half woman and half fish. Sirens and mermaids are mythical beings that Magritte and Robbe-Grillet "paint" in order to bring them to the surface of consciousness. They dredge up collective images that have been stored in the memory banks of language and libraries—language repositories being synchronic and diachronic storehouses of knowledge. However, Robbe-Grillet is more interested in the production of meaning than in the recovery of meaning. Like Magritte, he takes fragments of collective myth and information, plays with these fragments, turns them around and upside down, and deflates common sense—which all too often imposes itself as the truth when in fact it is false—in order to produce new ways of perceiving reality. Instead of the "Library of Babel," Borges's metaphor for the labyrinth of language, Robbe-Grillet has chosen a canning factory in which salmon and mermaids are canned for public consumption. In "Sur le choix des générateurs," Robbe-Grillet says:

> In the use of these themes (whose purpose is generative) . . . there is no submission to social codes—either to the code of values or to the narrative code—on the contrary, it is a work of deconstruction on elements carved out of the code—elements that are labeled as mythical, dated, situated, nonnatural, exposed to the light of day, instead of bathing obscurely in their original plasma; moreover, the function of the established order is to make them pass unnoticed, without a hitch, as though they had always existed and would continue forever. It is this element, precisely, that defines Nature.
>
> (2:160–61)

In *La Belle Captive* the bankrupt values of the establishment and the myth of an inviolate nature are under attack. The "abandoned" canning factory is Robbe-Grillet's metaphor for this "natural" system, and it is this labyrinth that is being explored by one of the narrators. Magritte's picture of the "salmon" factory, as interpreted by Robbe-Grillet, is *The Revelation of the Present* (plate 53). It depicts a giant index finger poking through a partly demolished building on the water's edge. Even as we note these details, the title evokes the narrative tense of the "nouveau roman," that is, the present. The factory that cans fish and the creative process that produces text are both sources of pleasure: monetary for the businessman, gastronomic for the consumer, and intellectual for the reader. We should not forget that "best-sellers" are also consumed and discarded like refrigerators or eliminated like food. Today's best-seller ends up on tomorrow's garbage heap. In a consumer society there seems to be no difference between the production of books and the production of refrigerators. Both have a built-in entropy—a progressive degradation—that guarantees their obsolescence. The popular romances that are all cut from the same cloth provide one such example: they appeal to the coded expectations of a certain kind of reader. Robbe-Grillet's novels, like Magritte's paintings, expose the tastes of the consumer while devaluing the popular codes that give rise to them. In this sense, although their art is not overtly political, it is subversive. As Magritte avers, "Surrealism is revolutionary because it is the indomitable foe of all the bourgeois ideological values that are keeping the world in its present appalling condition" (*EC* 108).

Magritte and Robbe-Grillet subvert the West's controlling fantasy system. They do so not by destroying art but by turning its processes back on themselves, that is, by exposing society's structures and mythology. In *Fantasy: The Literature of Subversion* Rosemary Jackson argues that fantasy, in and of itself, is subversive because it provides alternative ways of imagining the structures of society and ideology. Insofar as fantasy appeals to the unconscious—to the feelings that society represses—Jackson concludes that the formal and thematic features of fantastic art are determined by our attempt to find a language for desire (62). If Freud is right, fantasies express libidinal drives toward pleasure, the libido being that part of the self which wrestles with the reality principle. (*Toward Pleasure* is the title of the Magritte painting with which part 4 of *La Belle Captive* begins; these are also the last two words of the novel itself.) The libido, the locus of desire, constantly strives to overcome the restraints of reality. Reflexive art constantly challenges the restraints of realism. Such art is subversive because it has different pleasures in mind than the ones sanctioned by society.

Because Western cultures place such heavy emphasis on buying, Magritte's and Robbe-Grillet's art underscores not the consumption of a text but the production of one. The goal of a literary work, says Barthes in *S/Z*, is to make the reader a producer of the text, not a consumer (4). Robbe-Grillet illustrates the production of meaning— one of the sources of the "pleasure of the text"—with Magritte's *The Master of the Revels* (*Le Maître du plaisir* [plate 63]), a painting that is worth describing in some detail. In the foreground, inside a room, is a baluster, like the one used to deflower Vanessa and to wound her brother, David (29). The baluster inside is connected by a tightrope to the smokestack of a factory outside, situated at the water's edge. But the "reality" of the factory is suspect: is it seen through a window, is it a painting on the wall of the room, or is it no more than a reflection in a mirror? The smokestack is as nebulous as the creature balancing on the tightrope. This "master" is none other than Magritte's bell (the grelot), which has grown legs and a head. Moreover, this living object is now on fire—a flaming performance that is dramatized further by a set of curtains framing the room.

In *Pour une théorie du nouveau roman* Ricardou notes that "flaming fiction" ("fiction flamboyante," as he calls it) defines the nouveau roman: it "illumines" the product and "consumes" itself in the process. It "enlightens" the reader even as it self-destructs (see *The Fanatics* [plate 16]). "Condemned repeatedly to rise up again, another, from its own ashes, it resembles the contradictory wearer of feathers that Mallarmé, by hypo-gram, takes pleasure in dislocating: fea-nix, Phoenix" (219). My English translation cannot render the full range of verbal play: "fire-naught" and Phoenix are too far apart for effective paronomasia. I have tried to approximate the French sound (*feu-nixe*, *le phénix*), though not the meaning, by playing on the word "feathers," hence "fea-nix." Fire (*feu*) is the origin of this delightful ambiguity of language. When we consider that fire, as we have seen, connotes pleasure and sexuality, then *The Master of the Revels* becomes the code image of the artist walking the tightrope between the creative act, the production of meaning, and consumption as a pleasurable activity. Viewed from a certain angle, Magritte's painting becomes an image of reified desire.

Beneath the reveler's tightrope, several steps connect the room inside with the factory outside. In addition to the sexual symbolism of steps that Freud and Derrida stress, there are also the sexual connotations of the bell, the fire, the baluster, and the smokestack. Says Derrida in *La Vérité en peinture*: "Ever since Jacob, each time we dream of a sexual act, it represents symbolically an ascent or a rapid descent. 'Stairs, ladders, a step or the rung on a ladder, going up as well as going down, are symbolic represen-tations of the sexual act (*Traumdeutung*)'" (193). The steps in *The Master of the Revels* resemble the steps in *The Difficult Crossing* (plate 8) and *The Birth of the Idol* (plate 57). The title of *The Ladder of Fire* (plates 14 and 15) provides the rungs for the symbolic ascent Derrida refers to. In *The Master of the Revels* production, consumption, and desire all contribute to the master's pleasurable performance. He is on fire.

Fire burns holes in the text, opens it up, invites audience collaboration. The reader/viewer has to perform his or her own balancing act, and, following the artist's example, he or she stages or reassembles objects, people, names, and places in unusual and unconventional ways. This is the *bricolage* so frequently referred to by the practitioners of the nouveau roman. In addition to assembling objects, they take snippets of myth and exaggerate them. They play with *doxa*, exposing its arbitrariness. They create works that are deliberately antinatural in order to emphasize the artificial. The artist's deviance is thus a departure from and even a flouting of the so-called natural codes, because, as Robbe-Grillet notes in "Sur le choix des générateurs," all nations and all religions, sooner or later, claim that their system of values is natural and God-given:

> For the first time, a mode of production announces itself as nonnatural; . . . the myth of the natural . . . has been used by the social, moral, and political order in order to establish and prolong itself. Bourgeois order, bourgeois morality, and bourgeois values were supposed to be natural, i.e., inscribed in the order of things, and were therefore just, innocent, and definitive. Narrative order was similarly viewed: it was not supposed to pose any problems concerning the origin and justification of its formal structures.
>
> (159–60)

Magritte's and Robbe-Grillet's art opposes all systems that emphasize their own inevitability. Their art subverts these established norms while advocating the nonnatural. Magritte's bowler-hatted man is his code image for the bourgeoisie. Moreover, it is bowler-hatted men who confine and interrogate Robbe-Grillet's unconventional narrator. The bowler hat and black coat thus remind us of Joyce's H. C. E., the initials for Everyman—here comes everybody. Magritte's faceless bourgeois also resembles W. H. Auden's "Unknown Citizen," driving car after car down the wreck-strewn roads of Jean-Luc Godard's *Week-end*.

In his painting, Magritte deliberately obscures the faces of these "straw men" precisely because they have no identity. This "man of the crowd" has a body dressed like all the other bodies—people dressed in mass-produced garments bought in collective department stores. These men, like the men in *The Time of the Harvest* (plate 40), all resemble each other in appearance and expression. They dress alike and they think alike. They have no *parole*. All they do is reproduce encratic language. When Foucault asserted "the death of man" in *Les Mots et les choses*, he had in mind this loss of individuality and identity. "Man is dead" because language does not originate in him. Man is only the vehicle, a transmitter of social clichés and encoded values. It is not surprising, in view of their shared ideas, that Magritte should write fan letters to Foucault, since Magritte was an avid reader of books by philosophers, or that Foucault should write *Ceci n'est pas une pipe*, the essay in which he discusses Magritte's "use of words" (the title of one of the "pipe" pictures) in relation to language, structuralism, and painting.

Magritte's distrust of the bourgeoisie, even though he himself lived and dressed like a bowler-hatted man, has always been pronounced. This explains why he paints a man's face—the face is every man's identity—obscured by an apple (*The Son of Man*) or by a pigeon (*The Man in the Bowler Hat*). Magritte has painted man's anonymity, his void, his emptiness, because, in essence, every bourgeois has the same face, and each one can be identified by the ready-made. Magritte's pronouncements on this matter are corrosive and aggressive. He goes beyond commonality to emphasize the stupidity, baseness, and duplicity of the bourgeois mind:

> We are merely the subjects of this so-called civilized world, in which intelligence, baseness, heroism, and stupidity get on very well together and are alternately being pushed to the fore. We are the subjects of this incoherent, absurd world in which weapons are manufactured to prevent war, in which science is used to destroy, to construct, to kill, to prolong the life of the dying, in which the most insane undertaking works against itself.
>
> (*EC* 103)

In this context, as Bruce Kawin points out, a patriarchal ideology is frequently mispresented as natural and its taboos construed as ethical truths. An art that violates sociopolitical boundaries often uses the same strategies that batter the limits of language (320). Thus, both Magritte and Robbe-Grillet take pleasure in deflating bourgeois mythology and in poking fun at the seriousness of so-called collective truth (see *Collective Invention* [plate 48]). Nevertheless, bourgeois values are still assembled in the "canning factories" of ideology—a mythology that is consumed, produced, and reproduced by "everybody": beautiful girls on the travel posters for exotic islands, fast automobiles being sold and driven by lush sirens who never grow old, "wide-bodied" hostesses to fly you to Dallas, or servile Oriental women to fulfill your dreams in Singapore. Mythic images are all around us, catering to our desires, our pleasures, and our lusts.

THE PLEASURE OF THE TEXT

Magritte dramatizes the link between public performance and the private self and, like Robbe-Grillet, explores the latent eroticism of the creative act. Of course, Freud was well aware of the sexual symbolism of writing, the releasing of liquid from a pen onto blank paper, an act that he describes in "Project for a Scientific Psychology." Derrida, in his study of Freud's "Project," interprets the word "Bahnung," a term referring to the economic relationships between various parts of the psyche, as a double image of the act of inscribing a text and of sexual penetration ("La Scène de l'écriture"). Since Freud, the sexual connotations of the creative act in terms of pleasure, penetration, or gestation have indeed become commonplace.

Magritte's 1936 drawing *White Magic* is thoroughly consistent with this sexual symbolism of the creative act: it depicts a seated and clothed man inscribing the word *écrire* ("to write") on the abdomen of a reclining woman, whose naked body has become "the body of his text." The pleasure that Barthes derives from all such "writerly" endeavors is prefigured in Magritte's pencil drawing in which he is literally writing the body. In this context, it is fitting that the figure in *The Master of the Revels*, who is "inflamed" by desire, should do his balancing act on the tightrope above the steps, between the phallic baluster and the phallic smokestack. For Magritte and Robbe-Grillet, pleasure proposes an experience that is not without erotic and ironic overtones.

The finger poking through the roof of Magritte's "factory" (*The Revelation of the Present* [plate 53])—the finger that is a smokestack—is the same finger that spells the letter *I* (dotted with a little bell) in the word *sIrène* (the painting is entitled *The Use of Words*). No wonder Robbe-Grillet's "factory" cans fish and sirens, be they drowned virgins or deflowered Vanessas (a Vanessa is also a rare butterfly that loves flowers!), and Derrida is no doubt right to link text and penetration with the economic relationships between various parts of the psyche.

There is as much pleasure, perhaps more, in eating a bird as in canning fish, as suggested by Magritte's painting *Pleasure* (plate 64). *Pleasure* shows a young girl eating a bird (this is the picture's alternate title) that she has picked from a "bird tree"—eating it feathers and all, as one might eat an apple. In Robbe-Grillet's novel, the interrogator asks the prisoner to explain the meaning of Vanessa devouring the fire-bird: "It is probably another sexual metaphor, like everything else" (132).

Another painting, *The Pleasure Principle* (plate 50), depicts a man dressed in a coat and tie sitting at a table. His right hand rests on the table, and his fingers are poised as though to reach for the stonelike object that looks like a meteorite. The man's head has been replaced by a pure, glowing incandescence—the principle of pure pleasure and consciousness. Says Magritte: "Our mental universe is sunlit with pleasure that we have chosen like a sun to guide us" (*EC* 223). The arm is the link between the meteorite on the table and the glowing head that is as bright as the sun. Since the sun, as Magritte has noted, is our origin (*EC* 122), a meteorite may be viewed as a fragment from the big bang, the original explosion with which the universe began. The evolution of life from its earliest beginnings has culminated in humanity, a conscious being capable of experiencing pleasure as well as "reflecting" on pleasure.

According to astrophysicists, the universe everywhere is composed of identical chemical elements and compounds. The history of the universe, says Hubert Reeves, is the story of matter organizing itself along specific lines: particles, nuclei, stars, atoms, molecules, cells, and living beings all belong to the same evolving continuum. From the initial big bang, during a period of approximately fifteen billion years, there has been a "logical" organization of matter to produce life. Humans are made literally of star dust, and human consciousness is the triumphant end product of the organization of matter. Since consciousness is normally not visible, an art form that can materialize it is indeed magical. *The Pleasure Principle* re-creates, symbolically, the primordial emergence of organized matter. In the words of Teilhard de Chardin, this emergence of organized matter has become a flood carrying "the living mass ever onward toward consciousness" (147).

The world as we know it has evolved trees that produce fruit, but why not also trees that produce birds? Magritte takes pleasure in exploiting the free field of creative possibilities outside the range of the "normal." If these possibilities are freed from their bonds and allowed to develop, a new reality emerges. It is the pleasure of creating different combinations that attracts and fascinates both Magritte and Robbe-Grillet. *The Pleasure Principle* links the artist's imagination with a universal force. The painting's incandescence, its fire, transmits (through the position of the arm and hand) to matter a primal urge of sexuality and pleasure that leads to the ultimate creative act: *The Beautiful Captive*, that is, reflexive art and the self-awareness of the text.

In *The Mind of the Novel* Kawin points out that the problem of self-awareness depends on two factors: "Of what is one aware? and whose awareness is it? These questions cancel each other out in the intuition that the self exists. All levels of consciousness are capable of suddenly reducing to this luminous point" (15). *The Pleasure Principle*, when joined with *The Beautiful Captive* (plate 27), gives us the intuition of consciousness as a creative act that points to itself as a creative act. This is the luminous point.

When we recall that Robbe-Grillet begins his novel with the falling meteor, that the novel devotes itself to the pursuit of pleasure, that Robbe-Grillet's interest is in the story of telling and not in telling a story—then we realize the consciousness of the creative act and the reflexive structures that transmit this consciousness to the reader constitute the artist's goal. Magritte pronounces, "Thought is light" (*EC* 391). This is "the pleasure principle" of writing, of "the writerly" text, of "flaming fiction." Magritte's painting *The Pleasure Principle* is its code image.

When we recall that the stone, the egg, and the cell are generative sources, when we recall that the stone with the V-shaped mark on it connotes the statue of pleasure, Victorious Vanadis and Vanquished Vanadis, when we recall the "desirable virginity" (another *v*) of the captive and the sexuality of writing—then we perceive the suggestive "aura" of *The Pleasure Principle*, which begins part 3 of Robbe-Grillet's text. Besides, Magritte himself links painting with pleasure, with light, and with eroticism.[10]

---

10.   In explaining his artistic stance vis-à-vis futurism, Magritte says: "I had before my eyes a provocation attacking common sense, which annoyed me greatly. It [futurism] was for me the same *light* [my emphasis] that I discovered, a long time ago, when emerging from the crypts of the old cemetery, where, as a child, I spent my vacation. I *painted* [my emphasis] a whole series of inspired futurist pictures. However, I don't think I was an orthodox futurist, because the lyricism I wished to capture had an unchanging focus with no connection to artistic futurism. It was a pure and powerful feeling: *eroticism*" [my emphasis] (quoted in Waldberg, *René Magritte*, 86). Magritte's verbal linkage of light, painting, and eroticism in an existential context of death and in an ontological context of play illumines the meaning of his art. His clandestine games with his little girl friend; the dark tomb; the bright sunshine; the Sunday painter who, says Magritte, "revealed" to him his vocation as an artist—together these explain the "eroticism" he refers to with respect to futurism and art in general. Ultimately,

Pleasure is indeed an essential dimension of the "writerly" text. In pursuit of "bliss" (in *The Pleasure of the Text*, Barthes calls it *jouissance*), Robbe-Grillet has included five Magritte paintings oriented "toward pleasure": *The Depths of Pleasure* (plate 30), *The Pleasure Principle* (plate 50), *The Master of the Revels* (*Le Maître du plaisir* [plate 63]), *Pleasure* (plate 64), and *Toward Pleasure* (plate 69). Says Magritte: "When we deliberately chose pleasure as life's supreme goal, we already had twenty years of surrealism behind us" (*EC* 223). The last sentence of Robbe-Grillet's text echoes Magritte's preoccupation: "Once more something urges me out of myself toward pleasure" (156). The novel begins with a falling stone and ends with the word "pleasure." *A la recherche du temps perdu* ends with the word "time." It would seem that pleasure is as significant a leitmotif for Robbe-Grillet as time was for Proust. We should also keep in mind Barthes's emphasis on *jouissance* in *The Pleasure of the Text*, a form of bliss that Robbe-Grillet and Magritte both pursue in order to "possess" their beautiful captives. Robbe-Grillet's narrator says: "The hunt resumes once again. Already, at the far end of the long corridor, enclosed in a remote room behind parallel, vertical bars, immobile, the beautiful prisoner, as yet untouched, smiles at me inexplicably from her cage" (156).

It is perhaps significant that the adjectives "vertical" and "immobile"—adjectives that are used to describe the falling stone, the bars of the cell, and Anne-Marie; adjectives that appear in the opening and closing paragraphs of the novel—should reinforce the secret connection between stone and woman. Robbe-Grillet's descriptions support Magritte's portrayal of unusual affinities between the animate and the inanimate. Once again Anne, the mother, and Marie, the virgin, emphasize the self-restoring level of the text, a text that every reader approaches anew, as though it were virginal and "untouched."

We have already discussed the rock inside the room of *The Invisible World* (plate 3). Magritte's *Visible World* (plate 20) depicts a smaller version of the rock set on a table covered with a white tablecloth. The table is on a sandy beach and beyond it are the sea, the sky, and the horizon. Directly above the rock, in the night sky, is a crescent moon—the same crescent moon that is visible above the bird-mountain in *The Domain of Arnheim* (plate 10) and beyond the curtains in the painting entitled *Anne-Marie and the Rose* (plate 77), the last illustration in Robbe-Grillet's novel. *Anne-Marie and the Rose*, although deliberately trite, sums up Robbe-Grillet's and Magritte's themes: the dramatization of art and the imagination, woman as mythic goddess, lunar cycles, nature's affinities, the sky, the moon, the sea, the rose, eggs, and stones. *Anne-Marie and the Rose*

---

all of Magritte's paintings illustrate this "pure and powerful feeling": *The Beautiful Captive*, *The Invention of Fire*, *The Pleasure Principle*, and *White Magic* are four examples, among many, whose content and titles clearly illustrate this idea. Robbe-Grillet's work, like Magritte's, is also full of eroticism. In an interview with Michel Rybalka, published in *Le Monde*, 22 Sep. 1978, Robbe-Grillet says: "What Interests Me Is Eroticism" (7).

is an appropriate ending to the painterly and writerly "pleasure" that both artists have been pursuing.

The novel's four parts are untitled, but each section begins with an illustration. The first three pictures depict a stone, among other things, while the fourth one depicts a landscape, two men, and a bell. The first, *The Castle of the Pyrenees*, represents the huge falling rock. The second, *The Visible World* (plate 20), depicts a stone on a table. The third, *The Pleasure Principle* (plate 50), in addition to the man with the luminous head, depicts another stone on a table. The fourth, *Toward Pleasure* (plate 69), depicts two men in black hats and coats, a landscape, the bell, and a curtain. In addition to the novel's four parts, there is the title itself, which subsumes the text and the paintings and provides the link between desire and art. The fair captive is both the source and goal of all pleasure.

Nevertheless, there are "forbidden pleasures" (see *The Forbidden Universe* [plate 62]), as certain titles, the content of the paintings, and the text imply. These pleasures may be censored or repressed by the forces of "law and order." *The Invention of Fire*, described in the novel as "the bride stripped bare on a machine" (132); *Black Magic* (plate 56), depicting a naked woman with a dove on her shoulder; and *The Forbidden Universe*, depicting a mermaid reclining on a loveseat, with her eyes closed, holding a rose—all these paintings, titles, and texts denote or connote some form of religious, social, or sexual transgression.

"The bride stripped bare on a machine," like *The Forbidden Universe*, is an emblem of desire. The fascist types who inhabit the corridors of power, and who have repressed desire by incarcerating our narrator in the cell of the labyrinth, are dealing with an explosive situation. For desire is explosive. Gilles Deleuze and Félix Guattari affirm this point eloquently in *Anti-Oedipus: Capitalism and Schizophrenia*: "There is no desiring-machine capable of being assembled without demolishing entire social sectors" (xxiii). Robbe-Grillet renders the demolition of the social sector literally: the city is in ruins, even as Fantômas returns to the scene of the crime offering a rose. The painting entitled *The Backfire* (plate 75) is Magritte's and Robbe-Grillet's offering. It is the flesh-colored rose of desire, the antidote to fascism and repression—the two forces that Deleuze and Guattari denounce with such playful vehemence. However, in Magritte's canon the rose connotes not only desire but also woman, pleasure, and eroticism. The cultural revolution advocated by Deleuze and Guattari has and is being pressed forward by Magritte and Robbe-Grillet. Since the body is a "desiring-machine," all the connotations of "the bride stripped bare" reinforce the authors' efforts to subvert a repressive bourgeois morality. In Robbe-Grillet's film *La Belle Captive*, the fascist soldiers—dressed like SS men but without Nazi insignia—assert deadly power over the actions of people trying to be free and spontaneous.

La Belle Captive is subversive because society, as we know it, represses desire. Indeed, Freud's analysis of "the pleasure principle," as it is transformed into "the reality principle," confirms this thesis. Civilization and its discontents may in fact be traced to the delay of immediate pleasure for the sake of future satisfactions. In Gide's *Les Nourritures terrestres* are not the greatest pleasures the pleasures that have been delayed? In 1893, the year of his visit to North Africa, Gide was certainly the child of a Protestant work ethic—the living incarnation of Freud's theory. In the desert Gide learned that toil, effort, and guilt could be replaced by joy, spontaneity, and the absence of repression. "Satisfactions, I seek you!" The desert taught him how to shed the "reality principle" in favor of "the pleasure principle," an experience that was to generate the novel *L'Immoraliste*.

L'Immoraliste in fact rejects the proposition that civilization should be based on the subjugation of sexuality. It refuses the premise that renunciation and delay in satisfaction are necessary for progress. It questions the idea that happiness must be subordinate to the discipline of work as a full-time occupation. It does not accept the sacrifice of the libido as a precondition for culture.

Who has heard the message? The surrealists, perhaps more than others, as Breton's railings against the work ethic and his advocacy of *l'amour fou* ("mad love") attest.[11] Furthermore, society, as Herbert Marcuse points out, not only represses desire but turns desire against itself. Society has managed to persuade itself that repression is desirable, that subservience to work is progress, that division of labor is necessary, and so forth, all for the sake of "security and happiness." The rhetoric of persuasion is everywhere. Joy is repressed so that work may triumph. Amid the ruins that Robbe-Grillet describes, Magritte's finger (see *The Revelation of the Present* [plate 53]) reminds us of the omnipresence of desire and pleasure, however repressed. Magritte's art and Robbe-Grillet's novel exhort us away from repression and "toward pleasure."

POINT OF VIEW

Depending on your point of view, pleasure is the appealing or corrosive message of *La Belle Captive*. Indeed, there is pleasure in one of the murderer's crimes. It is pleasure that he carries with him in his suitcase. It is pleasure—the rose—that Fantômas holds in his hand (*The Backfire* [plate 75]). It is this "forbidden content" of the narrative that bothers the guards (as well as bourgeois and Party readers), who are dressed in long, black, carefully buttoned coats and black bowler hats. The guards interrogate the narrator concerning inconsistencies in his story by pointing to the gaps and contradictions in the text:

11. See André Breton, *L'Amour fou.*

[*Interrogator:*]	Are you quite sure that this story is about a bird and not about a big fish? . . .
[*Narrator:*]	No. If the word "salmon" was mentioned it can only be in order to evoke the flesh-colored rose that has been referred to several times. The only fish involved would be the girl herself, when the sailors brought her back to the surface, caught in their fishing nets.

(109)

The narrator covers his tracks, blurs the text, lies, confuses the reader. At one point he cries out: "But what am I saying? And to whom?" (154). To whom indeed, if not the reader? He is certainly not addressing his interrogators, for their questions are as disjointed as his answers. Such narrative dislocations and disruptions make it impossible to read metafiction in any conventional way. It undermines itself as it evolves—a deliberate, systematic destruction (hence the ruined city) of the natural order of storytelling. The narrator tries to defend himself, lies, invents new episodes that unfold seemingly without rhyme or reason. They certainly have no logic in the classical narrative sense, and the reader who reads by the old standards is disoriented, bored, disturbed by a text that seems to go nowhere and whose leaps in time and space contradict all the "laws" of good narration. Outwardly, the book is as incoherent as Magritte's paintings. But it has an inner coherence, a secret thread of meaning that is thematic rather than chronological. A whole emerges that accounts for the contradictions, the gaps, and the repetitions. What we get is a synchronism comparable to a retrospective of Magritte's works that allows for themes, connections, and meanings to emerge from the inchoate nature of the subject matter.

La Belle Captive, like Beckett's *Unnamable*, has no discernible plot, few namable characters, no particular setting, no clockable time. All it has is a shifting voice, speaking in the continuous present, that eventually becomes conscious of itself. The text has an awakened identity like the awakening of the narrator before relapsing into his drugged sleep (*The Cape of Storms* [plate 49]). In elaborating self-conscious discourses, both Beckett and Robbe-Grillet have been accused of killing the novel. However, as Kawin points out, neither writer is obscuring the function of literature or composing death dirges (280). Rather, both writers are awakening language from a drugged sleep, infusing it with new potential. This art talks about itself so that it can be itself. The parameters of its self-consciousness duplicate the parameters of the audience's world by stressing the function of language art as a system within the limits of consciousness.

Without a doubt, narrative displacement, spatial overlapping, and character doubling create ambiguity and contradiction. Typical of such equivocal relationships is the scene in which the soldiers in black have driven the narrator from the white corridors toward the cell in which he now finds himself. Since the narrator can see only the back of his head in the mirror, even though he is looking at himself face forward, he says it is he himself, probably, but he can't be sure (54). The text, with its allusion to Poe, reproduces the mystery of Magritte's *Not to Be Reproduced* (plate 24). On the mantelpiece lies a copy of *The Narrative of Arthur Gordon Pym*. It is perhaps interesting to note, although the discrepancy is to be expected, that in Poe's oeuvre it is William Wilson, not Arthur Gordon Pym, who sees his double in a mirror.

The absent narrator has become an anonymous narrator who in time becomes the false doctor. Eventually the false student's black notebook ends up in the narrator's hands. This notebook contains the original title—*Propriétés secrètes du triangle*—of Robbe-Grillet's novel *Souvenirs du triangle d'or*, portions of which have been incorporated into *La Belle Captive*. The student's "black notebook" (the code word for eroticism—as opposed to "white" and innocence) describes the properties of triangles, circles, and lines in exactly the same way *Souvenirs* does. Are we to assume that the false student is Robbe-Grillet's double? Perhaps. In any case, the questioning of the narrator by the two bowler-hatted interrogators frequently sounds like the text interrogating the reader, trying to trip him or her up with false details, dead ends, and blind alleys—different aspects of the textual labyrinth. At other times the text narrates itself, autonomously, as though it had a mind of its own, an independence vis-à-vis its author and the reader that is part of an intentional dialectic. Robbe-Grillet compares his new writing to conventional writing:

> The traditional narrative can always be viewed as an expression of meaning: tyrannical, totalitarian, devouring; all the narrative elements must work together to affirm it. The modern work, on the contrary, presents itself as unmarked space that is crisscrossed by multiple and changing meanings; besides, within the work's moving patterns of meaning, meaning is less important than the fact that it circulates, slides, and shifts.[12]

Although the decentered narrator is continuously evicted from cell to beach to café to the hallways of the labyrinth, the implied author continues to function from sentence to sentence. However, he no longer has any attributes. In *Le Voyeur* almost everything can be attributed to the consciousness of the traveling salesman who moves about the island and the narrative voice that accompanies his displacements. In *La Belle Captive*, even though the narrators are multiple, the implied author is always there despite the constantly shifting narrative voices. The role of the implied reader is to trace their displacements—this decentering of the conventional hero and conventional

---

12.   Quoted in Fano, "L'Ordre musical chez Alain Robbe-Grillet" 1:176.

narrative voice—from character to character, from gesture to gesture. As a result, the role of the audience has never been more active. We conclude that all the narrative elements, all the scenes, all the events, all of the instruments and characters are simultaneously narrative voices and narrated objects.

Insofar as the text of each nouveau roman is conscious of its diegesis; insofar as it reflects on its own procedures, structures, and displacements; insofar as it denounces the codes that it pretends to be using; insofar as it stresses the signifier over the signified—to that extent, each nouveau roman is in and of itself a theory of the novel. It seems to have a mind of its own that functions independently of its author, even though he or she is nevertheless always "there."

Robbe-Grillet's arrangement of Magritte's paintings thus serves a triple function: the paintings illustrate the theory of the nouveau roman; they highlight the author's "personal values"; and, as we have seen, they serve as generative catalysts for the author, the narrative, and the narrator(s).

THE MURDERER THREATENED

The Murderer Threatened (plate 4) derives from a scene in Louis Feuillade's *Fantômas* of 1912. It depicts two figures concealed by the doorway, armed with strange weapons, watching the "murderer," who is dressed in a business suit. *Fantômas*, the film, was based on the thirty-two-volume series written by Pierre Souvestre and Marcel Allain, each of whom wrote alternate chapters. Both Magritte and Robbe-Grillet seem fascinated by the character of Fantômas. *The Backfire* is an almost literal transposition from a cover of one of the novels: Magritte substitutes a rose for the dagger in Fantômas's hand. Since Fantômas can pass unseen through matter, he is the link between the inside-outside dialectic and the simultaneity that both Magritte and Robbe-Grillet pursue. Fantômas is everywhere. Because he defies the establishment and subverts its order, both Magritte and Robbe-Grillet admire his energy and cunning.

Cunning aside, what is the text of *La Belle Captive* saying, and why does the narrator return with a rose in his hand to recover the doctor's bag—the attaché case that has been left in the room of "the murderer threatened"? And why does the narrator, if he is not the murderer, comment on the false details reported in *Le Globe*—details that shift the reader's attention back to the painting of *The Murderer Threatened*—the fourth in the series—after the first three depicting stones, and just before *The Flowers of Evil* depicting the flesh-colored woman-statue holding the flesh-colored rose?

Each room of the canning factory (and the text) contains an object, be it a rose, a stone, or an apple—objects that are also textual indexes. The room portraying the stabbed mannequin, by its very complexity, sets up resonances that echo throughout the text. It matters little that Robbe-Grillet's narrative contradicts details in the paintings or adds to them since the pictures are subverted in the same manner that reality is contradicted. The three men looking in the window of *The Murderer Threatened* are not mentioned in the text and are replaced by a woman dressed in a diaphanous, white lace gown—like the nightgown of the woman in the film (*La Belle Captive*). In the text the bowler-hatted man is holding not a club but a baluster. Robbe-Grillet invents the sound of the phonograph that the young man is listening to. The narrator says it is replaying the woman's cry. The cry in turn animates the painting and the mannequin, which becomes a "real" woman. Although there is no sewing machine in the picture, the narrator tells us that the phonograph's age is the same as the sewing machine's.

Considering the subsequent allusions to tables, scalpel, captive, cane, umbrella, dissection, black hearse, and so forth, the sewing machine must be Lautréamont's. But why was the mannequin stabbed, and why was she chained to a metal bed (an intertextual reference to *Glissements progressifs du plaisir*) that is "at least as old as the sewing machine" or the phonograph (20)? Who is playing "forbidden" games? Robbe-Grillet, certainly, since he is toying with the reader, providing tantalizing tidbits from conventional thrillers and then undermining the reader's aroused expectations through contradiction and proliferation of detail.

Of what strange *Blow to the Heart* (plate 45) is the mannequin the victim, and why does the presumed murderer metamorphose into a brother (David), the incestuous son of Lady H-G? Why does the mannequin become Vanessa, the deflowered and drowned virgin who is then transformed first into a mermaid and then into the goddess Vanadis (Victorious and Vanquished), and so on? The reader staggers through this labyrinth of metamorphoses that are carefully rehearsed, cast, retold, and presented at the Night Palace, the Opera, the Temple, the beach café, the prison, and the canning factory.

The actors in this drama are stones, birds, fish, flowers, people, and language. Each object is a clue to something else in this pseudo–murder mystery wherein nothing is what it seems to be and everybody is wearing a mask. Why does the false doctor wear a disguise, and what is the narrator hiding? Nothing. Nothing at all, at least not in the mimetic or symbolic sense. The text is no more a mirror of reality than Magritte's paintings are. The text destroys itself, progressively, thereby emphasizing the writerly process as a systematic self-annihilation. Unlike the canned fish, the text refuses to be consumed. Moreover, the canning factory is as false as the false doctor or the false student, or as imaginary as the mermaids. The victim is reality, and the murderer is the artist. The sleuth is the audience, "the murderer on my trail," who must retrace the stages of the creative act, who must listen to the cry emanating from the false gramophone, who must also "violate" language and "kill" reality in order to grasp the significance of the transformations that have taken place—transformations that, at the end of each of the four parts, always emphasize the writerly process.

Part 1 ends with the narrator looking into his room—a room that is simultaneously inside and outside. He contemplates the mirror, the table, and "the fanatical temple [i.e., the text] whose outline I painfully retrace, day after day, through the retelling, the contradictions, and the gaps" (44).

Part 2 ends with the narrator's drugged dream, reproduced as Magritte's *Cape of Storms* (plate 49), a painting that depicts a man asleep in a wooden chest. In the background is a giant boulder on an empty horizon. The narrator has become the doctor, who, on his way to the abandoned factory, plans to leave his "victim" in one of the rooms. But he himself succumbs to the injection of the false student. The doctor, the narrator, and the text (the black notebook is the girl's) overlap as the passage becomes a drugged dream—a dream that begins with the falling stone and ends with Anne-Marie.

The narrator—like Walter Naime, the hero in the film *La Belle Captive*—is now the victim of the doctor's experiments. The identities of the student, the doctor, and the narrator fuse. The personal *je* ("I") of the narrative voice once again becomes abstract: "Then it begins again: the muffled footsteps in the hallway, the sound of the louver slamming, the silence and the long, deserted beach, the stone falling, and so forth" (104). Each sound, event, and image condenses textual passages, recapitulates them, reminds the reader of the content of the coded messages, and sets the stage for new permutations, for the narrative polysemia that continues to evolve.

Part 3, like the first two parts, ends on a sequence emphasizing the movement of the text from the cell inside to the desolation and freedom of the beach outside. It is the calm after the storm, after *The Difficult Crossing* (plate 8 and plate 33). We have been witnessing the passage from realistic art to reflexive art. It's a crossing over from texts that once imitated reality to texts whose "inner awareness" now rivals the world they used to reflect. In *The Difficult Crossing* (both versions) we witness the "shipwreck" of conventional art forms. The baluster with the eye is now an object that sees. This self-consciousness of art is a textual reality speaking with an autonomous voice—a voice emphasizing independence from nature, calling attention to the audience's creative freedom.

The epitome of this independence from nature is *The Annunciation* (fig. 20), a painting that juxtaposes artificial objects with objects in nature: two balusters, a paper cutout, and a metallic curtain with sixteen cowbells attached to it dwarf the trees, rocks, and earth and obscure the clouds and the sky. Unnatural things dominate the painting. This intrusion of huge artificial objects in a setting that denies them may be construed as "the annunciation" of "the liberator" (*The Liberator* [fig. 21]), that Magrittean figure holding a bejeweled candelabrum that bears the face of Scheherazade—another beautiful captive who is also a consummate weaver of reflexive tales. The liberator's symbolic key, glass, bird, and pipe are emblazoned on the man's torso—a torso that looks like one of Moses's tablets. This "annunciation" and this "liberator" embody the whole system of Magrittean values that we have been discussing. After "the difficult crossing," after "the birth of the idol"—be she or it bird, baluster, or captive—new modes of perception and apprehension of the world are theoretically possible. These new modes should allow us to control, reject, and transcend the duplicity and the stupidity of the bourgeois mind denounced by both Magritte and Robbe-Grillet.

Part 4 ends with a resumption of "the hunt"—the hunt for meaning, for a new captive, a new text, new and different pleasures. Throughout this relentless pursuit, nothing has been left standing, neither bourgeois values nor the text: all is abolished. Robbe-Grillet's description of the ruined city by the seashore corresponds to this undermining of reality and expectation: "the windows nonetheless light up the silhouettes of the rare buildings that remain standing in this wasteland of work yards and ruins" (141).

What *is* left standing is that other reality called art—that elusive entity that Magritte and Robbe-Grillet pursue through the labyrinth of things, words, images, and language. Through art and the artistic process, both men assert the primacy of the creative act to challenge nature and man's institutions. One of Robbe-Grillet's early essays was entitled "Nouveau Roman: Homme nouveau." Jacques Leenhardt compares this new man to a two-headed Janus looking both forward and backward (160–61). He is like the man in Magritte's painting *The Glass House* (plate 26), presenting a simultaneous view of his (Magritte's) face and the back of his head. Robbe-Grillet's fiction recapitulates the past, describes the present, and announces the future even as Magritte's painting *The Liberator* epitomizes the desire of both men to reshape the world in the image of "the beautiful captive."

This new art talks about itself in order to be itself. Its self-consciousness allows it to be simultaneously abstract and factual, absent and present, invisible and visible. It is both art and woman. Magritte's *Beautiful Captive* (plate 27), as a painting, denotes art and connotes woman. Robbe-Grillet's title and text denote woman and connote art. Together, painting and novel are the "false mirrors" of each other's intentions and fulfillments. "Elle, aile, belle" (she, wing, beautiful—the English falls short of poetic paronomasia) provide the necessary slippages of meaning. "She" is the *Idol* rising like the Phoenix from the ashes of *The Backfire* (plate 75). "She" is the picture of consciousness that links stone and woman by means of *The Pleasure Principle* (plate 50). The parthenogenetic egg generates the permutations and bifurcations of the artistic dialogue between text and image that is *The Beautiful Captive*.

FIGURE 4
The Flowers of the Abyss (*Les Fleurs de l'abîme*), 1928.
Oil on canvas, 54 × 73 cm. (21 × 28½ in.).
Private collection, Belgium.
(Photo: Giraudon, Paris)

FIGURE 5
The Lost Jockey (*Le Jockey perdu*), 1942.
Oil on canvas, 60 × 73 cm. (23½ × 29 in.).
Private collection, New York.
(Photo: Nathan Rabin, New York)

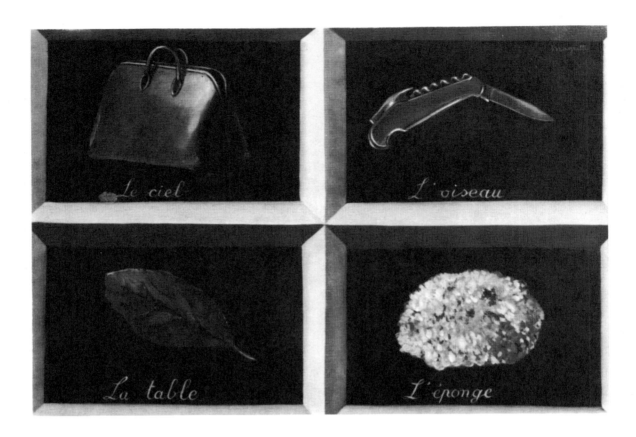

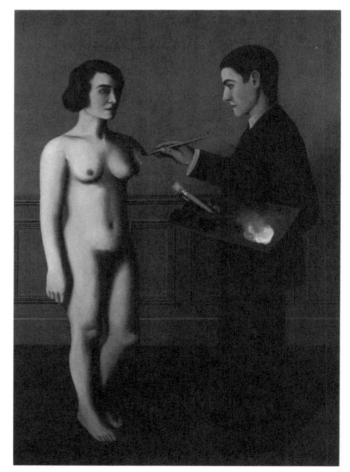

FIGURE 6
The Interpretation of Dreams (La Clef des songes), 1930.
Oil on canvas, 37 × 56 cm. (14½ × 22 in.).
Sidney Janis Gallery, New York.
(Photo: Geoffrey Clements, New York)

FIGURE 7 (*right*)
Attempting the Impossible (Tentative de l'impossible),
1928. Oil on canvas, 116 × 81 cm. (41½ × 32 in.).
Galerie Brachot, Brussels and Paris.
(Photo: Eril Landsberg, New Jersey)

FIGURE 8 (*opposite*)
The Art of Living (L'Art de vivre), 1967.
Oil on canvas, 65 × 54 cm. (25⅝ × 21¼ in.).
Private collection.

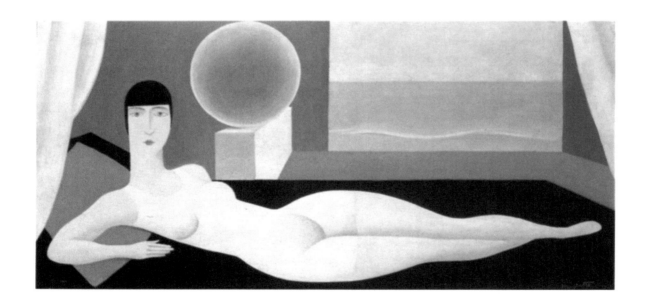

FIGURE 9 (*opposite, top*)
Three Nudes in an Interior, 1923. Oil on board,
56 × 60 cm. (22 × 23½ in.). Private collection.

FIGURE 10 (*opposite, bottom*)
Bather (Baigneuse), 1925. Oil on canvas, 50 × 100 cm.
(19½ × 39½ in.). Musée des Beaux-Arts,
Charleroi. (Photo: E. Dulière, Brussels)

FIGURE 11
*Bather Between Light and Darkness (La Baigneuse du
clair au sombre)*, 1935 or 1936. Oil on canvas,
89 × 115 cm. (35 × 45⅝ in.). Private collection.

FIGURE 18 (*opposite*)
Evening Falls (*Le Soir qui tombe*), 1964.
Oil on canvas, 160½ × 114 cm. (63¼ × 44⅞ in.).
Private collection.

FIGURE 19
The Traveler (*Le Voyageur*), 1935.
Oil on canvas, 55 × 66 cm. (21⅝ × 26 in.).
Private collection, Brussels.

FIGURE 20

The Annunciation (*L'Annonciation*), 1930.
Oil on canvas, 116 × 146 cm. (45½ × 57½ in.).
Tate Gallery, London.

FIGURE 21 (*opposite*)
The Liberator (*Le Libérateur*), 1947.
Oil on canvas, 99 × 79 cm. (39 × 31⅛ in.).
Los Angeles County Museum of Art, Los Angeles.

The Plot of the Novel

The following summary of *La Belle Captive* may be useful to readers who are not familiar with metafiction or the French New Novel. The contradictions, the discontinuities, the gaps in the text, and the proliferating voices can be disorienting to those who expect straightforward realism.

It may be useful to keep the four written parts of Robbe-Grillet's text in mind because the role of the paintings in the novel's diegesis is crucial: on the one hand, they comment on nouveau roman poetics, and on the other, they provide a necessary and parodic antidote to the text. There is a wry and comic tone to all the false details, exaggerations, stereotypes, and contradictions between any one picture and its textual counterpart.

PART I

The novel begins with a falling stone suspended above the waves of the sea (*The Castle of the Pyrenees*), then moves inside into different rooms where a woman (*Portrait of a Woman*), a stone (*The Invisible World*), and a variety of actors carry out strange and clandestine activities (*The Tomb of the Wrestlers*). A booby-trapped egg explodes (*The Domain of Arnheim*), and an idol (*The Idol*) is born. A third-person narrator describes a stone statue of a woman (*The Flowers of Evil*), the threatened murderer (*The Murderer Threatened*), and the birth of the false twins, David and Vanessa. The narrator alludes to David's incestuous and fratricidal tendencies, to the rape and drowning of Vanessa (*The Difficult Crossing*), to David's wound (*Memory*), and to the murderer's loss of memory; he then becomes a first-person narrator who goes to the opera and there gives the blonde Vanessa a summary of the plot of the performance entitled *The Idol* (*The Idol*), abducts her, and carries her limp body to a small room nearby, where he unlocks the door with a very hot key (*The Devil's Smile*, *The Ladder of Fire* [*I* and *II*]). A doctor makes his appearance (*The Dark Suspicion*). The narrator describes the sacred fire on the stage (*The Fanatics*). Later he finds himself walking among the ruins (*The Night Owl*) at the beach, crosses a bridge (*Pandora's Box*), buys a rose from a girl vendor, traverses the grounds that are being excavated, and, at dawn, finds himself in front of his own "dialectical" window (*In Praise of the Dialectic*) retracing the gaps and contradictions of his itinerary.

PART 2

Part 2 opens with Magritte's *Visible World*. Soldiers dressed in black uniforms and wearing heavy boots, leather belts, and black gloves push, shove, and jostle each other as they move through narrow corridors (*An End to Contemplation*). They seem to be pushing one man dressed in white pajamas (*Universal Gravitation*) into a room (*The Unexpected Answer*); they then close the door behind him. Perhaps the men are not soldiers after all; in any case, the corridors are now empty. The man (the first-person narrator) stands alone in the middle of the cell before a mirror. He has some difficulty recognizing himself since "they" have shaved his head. (*Not to Be Reproduced* depicts a man with hair—a comic contradiction—looking at himself in the mirror; only the back of his head appears there.) The narrator says that he resembles the picture of the murderer that appeared in the newspaper. This statement elicits a reader flashback to the picture of *The Murderer Threatened*.

There is an abrupt transition from the cell to a beachside café. The narrator sits down at a table, orders breakfast, and begins to read the newspaper. *The Globe* describes the face of the murderer and the position of the body, again echoing the painting of *The Murderer Threatened* (who has *The Face of Genius*). The narrator, noting that the body in the picture is not in the right place, interprets the body's displacement as an attempt at entrapment (*The Glass House*). The narrator raises his eyes in order to study a golden beauty playing ball on the beach. (*The Beautiful Captive* depicts, in addition to an easel, curtains, sky, and sea, a round sphere on the sand.) A black-haired coed sits down at an adjoining table on which there is a glass and a bottle of red lemonade. (*The Portrait*, which shows a bottle of red wine, provides a comic contrast to the word "lemonade" in the text.) The girl is a "belle adolescente pulpeuse." (*Philosophy in the Boudoir* provides yet another comic touch: the disembodied nightgown with flesh-colored breasts bulging through the cloth is the "illustration" of the sexy adolescent.) The narrator imagines that the girl sees him as a man resembling a surgeon with graying temples. The coed performs graceful movements above her head with her arms and hands that are reminiscent of the movements of the naked, chained, and captive woman performing in the night club of the film *Trans-Europ-Express* (*The Depths of Pleasure* depicts a naked woman embracing a life-size baluster). The narrator feels the penetrating gaze of the coed.

There is another abrupt transition from the beach café to the prison cell. The cell's door has a square spy window through which an eye is peering (*The False Mirror* depicts an eye). The spy window opens, and a man's bare arm passes through it. (*The Scars of Memory* depicts a hairy arm and hand holding a "hairy stone.") The narrator takes the black book (not the stone) from the extended hand. It is the black notebook of the false coed, who, still seated at the café table, continues to look at the narrator. (*The Difficult Crossing* shows an eye on a wooden baluster.) The coed's face resembles the face of a cover-girl on a glossy sex magazine—a code image signifying sex and desire. The narrator asks the girl to fetch his cigarettes from the black Cadillac parked at the curb. She looks at his orthopedic cane. (*Hegel's Holiday* depicts a glass of water balanced on top of an open black umbrella with a cane handle. The details of the painting provide a comic contrast to the orthopedic cane.) The narrator describes his disguise as belonging to a limping, inoffensive gynecologist or psychosomatician (comic invention reinforced by the painting *The Old Gunner*, which depicts a sitting and inverted merman with a peg leg embracing a young girl standing between his legs).

The coed gets the blue packet of cigarettes from the car's glove compartment, and the narrator offers her a drugged cigarette. (*State of Grace* depicts a bicycle on a smoking cigar; "la belle machine"—the bicycle—connotes the girl.) The girl faints, and the black waiter wearing the white jacket says something in Brazilian Portuguese (*The Central Story*). The narrator, pretending to be a doctor, asks the three men who have come to the girl's assistance to carry her to the "Caddy," which is described as a black-lacquered coffin. The narrator gives a detailed description of the golden dress and tanned body of the girl (appropriately illustrating his inner mood with the title *The Sirens' Song*). The narrator limps toward his car. (*Portrait* depicts a bowler-hatted man with a mustache and black coat using a foil as a blind man's cane.) The unconscious girl is placed in the car. The narrator gets in and begins writing in the car's log. When he is finished, he closes the covers of the notebook, which resound like a shot. A crowd of bathers is now looking in through the car windows. (*The Time of the Harvest* depicts bowler-hatted men looking into an empty room through an open window.)

Once again, without transition, the narrator finds himself in his cell in front of the closed spy window. (*Personal Values* depicts a bedroom, connoting the oneiric quality of the narrator's discourse.) The narrator hears the movements of the "soldiers" in the hall outside the cell. He opens the black notebook, whose title is *Propriétés secrètes du triangle*—the working title of Robbe-Grillet's *Topologie d'une cité fantôme*, published in 1976. The fine, regular handwriting in the notebook is that of a woman. There is a description of a triangle, circles, and bisecting lines (*The Elusive Woman*). There follows another abrupt transition to the Cadillac, which is now parked in a rundown and abandoned section of town. (*The Song of the Violet* depicts men of stone or stones that are men.) The narrator slits the girl's golden dress with his scalpel in order to reveal her tanned and naked body (*Figure Brooding on Madness*). The still unconscious and vulnerable girl is wearing only white deerskin boots and a golden cross around her neck. The narrator inserts a hypodermic needle into her right breast. (*The Blow to the Heart* depicts a rose with a dagger in lieu of a thorn; the dagger is the size of the rose.)

The narrator believes that his victim is looking at him with dilated pupils. (*The Agitated Reader* depicts a woman with bulging [horrified?] eyes reading a book; the "agitated reader" might well be reading *La Belle Captive*.) Another car parks behind the Cadillac and the narrator drives away. In his haste he cannot deliver his prey to the appointed place, and he barely has time to cast a glance (*The Eye*) at the mannequins dressed in white diaphanous gowns in the store windows.

The narrator crosses the bridge, but he does not stop to buy the last rosebud from the girl vendor. He passes in front of the Opera House and sees the spectators leaving. He drives along the seashore toward the abandoned factory, where he is determined to throw his false captive into the sea. (*Collective Invention* depicts a mermaid—with the legs of a woman and the head of a fish—lying on the beach.) The narrator feels a sharp pain in his right arm as the girl jabs him with her own hypodermic, which had been concealed in her boot. As he loses consciousness, the narrator again hears the footsteps in the corridor, the sound of the closing spy window, the silence of the deserted beach, the stone falling, and so forth. (*The Cape of Storms* depicts a man sleeping inside a wooden chest; a giant stone seems to hover above the wooden chest on the sienna-colored plain behind it.) Part 2 ends with the same dream motif that was present throughout part 1.

PART 3

The bowler-hatted men resume their interrogation of the prisoner, who is blinded by the spotlights. (*The Pleasure Principle* depicts a man seated at a table; his head and face are one luminous incandescent circle.) One interrogator, concerned about the discrepancy between the coed's white deerskin boots and the high-heeled shoe, speaks to the prisoner using the *vous* form. The narrator says that the high-heeled shoe was found by a bird at the base of the cliff. (*God Is Not a Saint* depicts a pigeon alighting on a woman's high-heeled shoe.) The interrogator wonders if it was not a fish instead of a bird that retrieved the sacred object (the shoe). No, says the prisoner: the only "salmon" was the color of the rose, and the only fish was the girl caught in the fisherman's net. (*The Presence of Mind* depicts a man flanked by a bird and a fish; they are all the same size.) The interrogator asks if the seaside factory isn't a cannery (*The Revelation of the Present* depicts a building with a finger poking through it like a smokestack) and then tries to trip the narrator on a variety of inconsistencies concerning his "story." The text of *La Belle Captive*, which is the narrator's story, is full of gaps and contradictions, slipping from one image and metaphor to another. The interrogator, who behaves like a classic realist reader, tries to fill the gaps in the story and to restore its plausibility. It would seem that Robbe-Grillet's text is being judged and challenged by the values of the bowler-hatted establishment—the bourgeoisie.

One of the interrogators asks about the apple the young girl was eating. (*The Listening Room* depicts a green apple occupying the entire space of a room.) Each room along the corridor (as in *The Tomb of the Wrestlers*, which contains a rose the size of the apple) displays a different object—the incriminating evidence. But what is the prisoner guilty of? He may well be guilty of murdering the classic realist novel. The purpose of the interrogation and the picture of the *The Murderer Threatened* now come into focus. At this juncture the text slides "involuntarily" into a description of the tanned beauty playing ball on the beach. (*Black Magic* depicts a naked woman by the seashore at the foot of the cliff with a pigeon on her shoulder.) The phantom bird (remember *God Is Not a Saint?*) comes back on stage (*The Entry on Stage* depicts a giant white bird in the starlit sky flying through the night above the sea) to accompany the birth of the idol on the sacrificial ship. (*The Birth of the Idol* depicts a stormy sea, a platform, and a human-sized baluster with a woman's arm.) Readers should flash back to *The Idol*, which depicts a flying stone bird, and *The Difficult Crossing*, which depicts a shipwreck; the props from this painting also figure prominently in *The Birth of the Idol*. The narrator describes a squall that washes a thirty-five-centimeter-long baluster up on the beach. It has the silhouette of a girl. The wind has also blown the girl's beach ball high into the sky. (*When the Hour Strikes* depicts the statue of a woman's torso on the sand; in the sky, above the sea, is a hot-air balloon.) The girl continues her tumbling somersaults on the sand, thus providing a humorous contrast between her antics and the immobility of the statue in the painting. The girl is holding an apple (*une pomme*) in her left hand (*sa paume gauche*); such paronomasia is the pretext for the next illustration, *The Great War*, which depicts a bowler-hatted man whose face is obscured by a green apple.

Next the narrator imagines that he entices the girl into a boutique nearby. In the change booth he thrusts a hollow needle into her upper buttocks and injects a narcotic, causing the girl to faint. (*Representation* depicts a mirror image of a woman's thighs, pubis, and abdomen.) The interrogator then asks about the seaweed, and the narrator answers that it is a metaphor for the girl's blonde hair. There follows a question-and-answer period concerning the sponge, the seashell, and the lemon. (*Familiar Objects* depicts five men in profile or semiprofile with objects suspended in front of their eyes; among these objects are a sponge, a seashell, and a lemon.) The narrator invents a "story" that confirms their "sexual contamination." This is enough to send the imagery of the text slipping into the sacrificial room, where the cruel ceremonies with the virgin and the baluster take place. (*The Forbidden Universe* depicts a reclining mermaid on a love seat; there is irony in her sensual pose and dozing unconcern.)

The cruel ceremonies continue at the cannery, where, after their immolation, the victims are cut up, canned, and sold as "spiced salmon." (*The Master of the Revels* depicts a rope stretched between the smokestack of a factory and a baluster inside a room; a flaming cowbell with a head, face, and legs performs a balancing act above five steps.) There is "pleasure" in the text, the title of the picture, the Freudian imagery, and the sexual connotations that accompany the juxtapositions. The narrator then describes the Opera House as a labyrinth for mythic representations presided over by the ancient divinity of pleasure: Victorious Vanadis and Vanquished Vanadis. The interrogator asks why Vanessa devours the bird of fire. (*Pleasure* depicts a woman devouring a bird she has just picked from a "bird tree.") The narrator says it is a sexual metaphor, like everything else, and then alludes to the ritual scenes with the chained captive in the nocturnal palace—"the rosy crucifixion" with the sponge and "la mariée mise à nue sur une machine"— allusions to art objects by Marcel Duchamp and Lautréamont. (*The Invention of Fire* depicts a naked woman on all fours on a balcony overlooking the sea; she is framed by a curtain and a human-sized baluster with a phallic head.) The following description evokes the black uniformed soldiers in the hallways of the labyrinth outside the rooms where the pleasure scenes are being enacted. (*The Human Condition II* depicts a beach scene similar to that of *The Beautiful Captive*: the oval object, the seascape, and the easel holding the canvas.) After the storm the beach is now quiet. The "demolition crew" (as opposed to the construction crew) has built a fire (*A Helpful Shove* depicts a night scene, a bird, and fire) on which the men are frying fish and chips. *The Exception* is a painting of a fish-cigar on a salmon-colored background; the tail of the fish is the burning end of the cigar: An impossible smoke and a comic ending.

PART 4

Part 4 opens with *Toward Pleasure*, which depicts two men, a curtain, grass, houses, trees, and sky; the ubiquitous oval cowbell is situated in the center of the painting on the grass. Part 4 echoes the themes of pleasure already announced in part 3. It is morning. The narrator awakens and describes the suburban landscape of bourgeois buildings that have been gutted by the explosion. The center of the explosion has left a crater that is filling with water from ruptured water lines. The black notebook describes the relative position of the buildings that have remained standing.

The indeterminacy of this text suggests that the explosion may refer to the eruption of the New Novel and that the devastated city may connote the classic realist novel. Meanwhile, the narrator says that he is sitting once again on the terrace of the beach café; this time he is wearing a white suit instead of the somber one he had on before. (*The White Man* depicts a man in a white suit reading *Le Matin*.) The naked woman standing behind the man in the white suit seems to be part of the pleasure leitmotif. The man at the café buys the latest edition of *Le Globe* (not *Le Matin*) and turns to the sex-crimes page, where he sees an enlarged photograph of the false doctor's attaché case. (*The Virgin's Chariot* depicts a valise on a hand mirror.) The narrator thinks about the interrogator's questions concerning the virginity of the missing victims and wonders if the attaché case contains apples or chloroformed sandwiches. The narrator describes his previous meeting in the corridor with the doctor, thereby eliciting a reader flashback to *The Glass House*.

The narrator describes the two men looking at each other; the painting and the text strongly suggest that the narrator and the doctor may be the same person. Nevertheless, the narrator asks the doctor if there is an exit. (*Poison* depicts a partly opened door through which a seascape is visible; a white cloud is floating into the room.) The doctor consults his pocket watch and leaves. The narrator wonders if the man wasn't one of the musicians on his way to the repetition; if so, the attaché case would contain a disassembled wind instrument. (*Threatening Weather* depicts a seascape with the statue of a woman's torso, a tuba, and a straight-backed chair situated in the sky where there might have been clouds.) The presence of the tuba in the picture generates the wind instrument inside the attaché case and the chair, since the narrator next sits down on a chair in order to ponder the situation. He notices blood flowing under the door and a white leather high-heeled woman's shoe lying on its side in the dark vermilion pool. The shoe, part of a costume for a performance at the Opera House, is decorated with precious stones. (*The Drop of Water* depicts the statue of a woman's torso covered with precious stones; behind her is a curtain, a stormy sky, and a wave-tossed ship floundering in the sea. The sea and ship remind us of *The Difficult Crossing* and *The Birth of the Idol*.) The selection of *The Drop of Water* reveals Robbe-Grillet's linking of the shoe and the woman: both are covered with precious stones and both are sacred objects. This identity legitimizes whatever reflections we may have concerning woman's sanguineous functions, lunar cycles, natural rhythms, and mythic rites. It also evokes Michelet's *La Sorcière* and two Magritte paintings, *The Blood of the World* and *La Saignée* (*The Bloodletting*). In any case, it was a man's arm that dropped the shoe through the spy window.

The judas now closes, but the narrator sees two eyes watching him through the slats. As though to bring us back to the text, a voice says: "Resume reading." The reader—like the narrator, since both are reading—returns to the passage in the black notebook that describes the return of the criminal to the city that is almost completely destroyed. He returns in order to retrieve the attaché case. The criminal is now holding a rose. (*The Backfire* depicts Fantômas with a rose in his hand dominating the Parisian landscape.) But the criminal has forgotten what to do with the rose and throws it into the river. A big bird appears in the sky, a daytime version, no doubt, of *The Entry on Stage*. The man picks up a black stone of volcanic origin with a V-shaped depression and "eyes." This stone evokes a reader flashback to all the previous stones, from *The Castle of the Pyrenees* to *The Scars of Memory*.

But all this is a fantasy account of the crime reported in the newspaper. The narrator puts it down, convinced that, except for the stone, there is no new element in the case (*The Man with the Newspaper*). "But what am I saying," says the narrator, "and to whom?" He concludes that all new questions are futile . . . and "the hunt" resumes, once more, along the interminable corridors. Inside the cell, the beautiful prisoner, still intact, smiles at him, generating images of the metal bed, the deserted beach, and the waves. This description reminds us of a haunting sequence in the film *Glissements progressifs du plaisir*. Once again something prompts the narrator to go out in search of pleasure (*Anne-Marie and the Rose*).

Robbe-Grillet's Note on the French Edition

To produce narration—however strange or antinatural—may in fact be a natural human activity, insofar as it has occurred at all times, everywhere, from ancient religious mythologies to our contemporary books of History, and by way of the fictitious adventures that children share, or the ones they elaborate in solitude. In this the novelist does no more than submit to the general rule; however, in the manner in which he composes his narrative, he knows, in ways that are no doubt more acute than most people's, that nothing can be natural: whether selecting a particular architecture, or a particular formal project, or a generative element, he must necessarily resign himself to reproducing the conventions put in place by his group's ideology, or else assume the absolute freedom of his own invention.

This disturbing mixture of a natural activity used in an arbitrary manner is illustrated, once again, in this book. While perusing the retrospective exhibition of one of his favorite painters, the writer immediately selects objects and stories. The figures come alive, the repetition of a theme becomes a diachronic development, the title of a painting emerges as a password . . .

Resemblance, however, is only part one of the adventure: whereas the writer initially accepted the pictures as generative impulses, soon the variable distance between them and the text—sometimes also the metonymical connection, or even opposition—becomes the principal parameter of the game. Thus, the reader-spectator is invited to participate (in order to create his own itinerary) in this circulation of meaning between the shifting organization of the sentence that allows us to see and the picture that narrates.

Alter, Robert. *Partial Magic: The Novel as a Self-Conscious Genre*. Berkeley: U of California P, 1975.

Baldensperger, Fernand. "Littérature comparée: Le Mot et la chose." *Revue de littérature comparée* 1 (1921): 7.

Barthes, Roland. *Essais critiques*. Paris: Seuil, 1964.

————. *Michelet*. Paris: Seuil, 1975.

————. *Le Plaisir du texte*. Paris: Seuil, 1973.

————. *The Pleasure of the Text*. Trans. Richard Miller. New York: Hill and Wang, 1975.

————. *S/Z*. Paris: Seuil, 1970.

————. "To Write: An Intransitive Verb?" *The Languages of Criticism and the Sciences of Man: The Structuralist Controversy*. Ed. Richard Macksey and Eugenio Donato. Baltimore: Johns Hopkins UP, 1970. 134–45.

Baudelaire, Charles. *Les Fleurs du mal*. 1857. Paris: Gallimard, 1961.

Bauer, George H. "The Robbe-Grillet / Magritte AV Frame; or, The Case of *La Belle Captive*." *Cream City Review* 7 (1981): 21–30.

Beckett, Samuel. *The Unnamable. Three Novels*. New York: Grove, 1955.

Berger, John. *Ways of Seeing*. New York: Penguin, 1972.

Borges, Jorge Luis. "The Library of Babel." *Labyrinths*. Ed. Donald A. Yates and James E. Irby. New York: New Directions, 1962. 51–58.

Braudel, Fernand, ed. *La Méditeranée: Les Hommes et l'héritage*. Paris: Arts et Métiers Graphiques, 1978.

Breton, André. *L'Amour fou*. Paris: Gallimard, 1937.

———. "Envergure de René Magritte." *Magritte*. Little Rock: Arkansas Art Center, 1964. N.p.

Caws, Mary Ann. *The Eye in the Text*. Princeton: Princeton UP, 1981.

Crichton, Michael. *Jasper Johns*. New York: Abrams, 1977.

Daly, Mary. *Gyn/Ecology: The Metaethics of Radical Feminism*. Boston: Beacon, 1978.

Deleuze, Gilles, and Félix Guattari. *Anti-Oedipus: Capitalism and Schizophrenia*. Trans. Robert Hurley, Mark Seem, and Helen R. Lane. Minneapolis: U of Minnesota P, 1983.

Derrida, Jacques. "Freud et la scène de l'écriture." *L'Écriture et la différence*. Paris: Seuil, 1967. 293–340.

———. *Glas*. Paris: Galilée, 1974.

———. *La Vérité en peinture*. Paris: Flammarion, 1978.

Eco, Umberto. *L'Oeuvre ouverte*. Trans. Chantal Roux de Bézieux. Paris: Seuil, 1965.

Eliade, Mircea. *The Sacred and the Profane*. New York: Harcourt, 1959.

Fano, Michel. "L'Ordre musical chez Alain Robbe-Grillet: Le Discours sonore dans ses films." Ricardou, *Robbe-Grillet: Analyse, théorie* 1: 173–213.

Foucault, Michel. *Ceci n'est pas une pipe*. Montpellier: Fata Morgana, 1973.

———. *Les Mots et les choses*. Paris: Gallimard, 1966.

———. *This Is Not a Pipe*. Ed. and trans. James Harkness. Berkeley: U of California P, 1982.

Frank, Joseph. "Spatial Form in Modern Literature." *Sewanee Review* 53 (1945): 221–41.

Freud, Sigmund. *Civilization and Its Discontents*. Ed. James Strachey. New York: Norton, 1961.

———. *The Standard Edition of the Complete Psychological Works*. Trans. James Strachey. Vols. 1–23. London: Hogarth, 1953.

Gablik, Suzi. *Magritte*. Greenwich, Conn.: New York Graphic Society, 1970.

Genet, Jean. *Le Balcon*. Paris: L'Arbalète, 1962.

Gibson, Walker. "Authors, Speakers, Readers, and Mock Readers." *College English* 11 (1950): 265–69.

Gide, André. *Les Faux-monnayeurs*. Paris: Gallimard, 1926.

———. *L'Immoraliste*. Paris: Mercure de France, 1902.

———. *Les Nourritures terrestres*. Paris: Mercure de France, 1897.

Gombrich, E. H. *Art and Illusion*. New York: Random, 1960.

Hammacher, A. M. *René Magritte*. New York: Abrams, 1974 [?].

Hazan, Fernand, ed. *Dictionary of Modern Painting*. Trans. Alan Bird, Lawrence Samuelson, Katie Kaplan, Mary Hart, and Barbara Marchutz. New York: Paris Book Center, n.d.

Hubert, Renée Riese. *Surrealism and the Book*. Berkeley: U of California P, 1988.

Iser, Wolfgang. *The Implied Reader: Patterns of Communication in Prose Fiction from Bunyan to Beckett*. Baltimore: Johns Hopkins UP, 1974.

Jackson, Rosemary. *Fantasy: The Literature of Subversion*. London: Methuen, 1981.

Jost, François. "Le Picto-roman." *Revue d'esthétique* 4 (1976): 58–73.

Kawin, Bruce. *The Mind of the Novel: Reflexive Fiction and the Ineffable*. Princeton: Princeton UP, 1982.

Krieger, Murray. *Ekphrasis: The Illusion of the Natural Sign*. Baltimore: Johns Hopkins UP, 1992.

Langui, Emile. *Magritte*. London: Marlborough Fine Art, 1973. [Catalogue.]

Lautréamont. *Les Chants de Maldoror*. Brussels: La Boétie, 1948.

———. *Oeuvres complètes*. Paris: G.L.M., 1938.

Leach, David, ed. *Generative Literature and Generative Art*. Fredericton, New Brunswick: York, 1983.

Leenhardt, Jacques. "Nouveau Roman et société." Ricardou, *Nouveau Roman: Hier aujourd'hui* 1: 155–70.

Magritte, René. *Écrits complets*. Paris: Flammarion, 1979.

Marcuse, Herbert. *Eros and Civilization: A Philosophical Inquiry into Freud*. New York: Vintage-Random, 1955.

Mariën, Marcel. *Magritte*. Brussels: Les Auteurs Associés, 1943.

Merriman, James D. "The Parallel of the Arts: Some Misgivings and a Faint Affirmation." *Journal of Aesthetics and Art Criticism* 31 (1972–73): 154–64, 309–21.

Michalczyk, John J. "Robbe-Grillet, Michelet, and Barthes: From *La Sorcière* to *Glissements progressifs du plaisir*." *French Review* 51 (1977): 233–44.

Michelet, Jules. *La Sorcière*. Paris: Garnier-Flammarion, 1966.

Mistacco, Vicki. Interview with Alain Robbe-Grillet. *Diacritics* 6 (1976): 35–43.

Mitchell, W. J. T. *Iconology: Image, Text, Ideology*. Chicago: U of Chicago P, 1986.

Morrissette, Bruce. *Intertextual Assemblage in Robbe-Grillet from "Topology" to "The Golden Triangle."* Fredericton, New Brunswick: York, 1979.

Nouveau Roman: Hier, aujourd'hui. Ed. Jean Ricardou and Françoise van Rossum-Guyon. Vol. 1, *Problèmes généraux*; vol. 2, *Pratiques*. Paris: UGE, 1972.

Oriol-Boyer, Claudette. "Les Cicatrices de la mémoire: Reproduction inter-dite. Propositions pour des lectures de *La Belle Captive*." *Recherches et travaux* (Grenoble) 14 (1976): 129–37.

Pinget, Robert. *Passacaille*. Paris: Minuit, 1969.

Poe, Edgar Allan. *The Narrative of Arthur Gordon Pym*. New York: Heritage, 1930.

Prince, Gerald. "Introduction to the Study of the Narratee." *Poétique* 14 (1973): 177–96.

Rabkin, Eric. *The Fantastic in Literature*. Princeton: Princeton UP, 1976.

Raillard, Georges. "Mots de passe: Quelques notes prises au cours d'une traversée difficile: *La Belle Captive*." *Obliques* 16–17 (1978): 203–12.

Reeves, Hubert. *Poussière d'étoiles*. Paris: Seuil, 1984.

Ricardou, Jean. *Pour une théorie du nouveau roman*. Paris: Seuil, 1971.

———. *La Prise de Constantinople*. Paris: Minuit, 1965.

———, ed. *Robbe-Grillet: Analyse, théorie*. Vol. 1 of *Roman/Cinéma*. Paris: UGE, 1976.

Riffaterre, Michael. "Describing Poetic Structures: Two Approaches to Baudelaire's 'Les Chats.'" *Yale French Studies* 36–37 (1966): 200–242.

Robbe-Grillet, Alain. *L'Année dernière à Marienbad*. Paris: Minuit, 1961.

———. "Après l'*Eden et après*." *Le Nouvel Observateur* June 26–July 5, 1970: 33–35.

———. "La Cible" [preface]. *Jasper Johns*. Paris: Centre de Culture Georges Pompidou, Musée National d'Art Moderne, 1978. [Catalogue of the Jasper Johns Exhibition, April 8–June 4, 1978, Paris.]

———. *Construction d'un temple en ruines à la déesse Vanadé*. Paris: Le Bateau-Lavoir, 1975. [Limited edition.]

———. "*L'Eden et après*: Début pour un ciné-roman." *Obliques* 16–17 (1978): 185–92.

———. *Glissements progressifs du plaisir*. Paris: Minuit, 1974.

———. *La Jalousie*. Paris: Minuit, 1957.

———. "Le Magicien: Projet de film." *Obliques* 16–17 (1978): 259–61.

———. "Nouveau Roman: Homme nouveau." Robbe-Grillet, *Pour un nouveau roman*, 113–22.

———. "Piège à fourrure (Début d'un projet de film)." *Minuit* 18 (1976): 2–15.

———. *Pour un nouveau roman*. Paris: Minuit, 1963.

———. *Projet pour une révolution à New York*. Paris: Minuit, 1970.

———. "Le Sadisme contre la peur." *Le Nouvel Observateur* 19 Oct. 1970: 47–49.

————. *Souvenirs du triangle d'or*. Paris: Minuit, 1978.

————. "Sur le choix des générateurs." Ricardou, *Nouveau Roman: Hier, aujourd'hui* 2: 157–62.

————. *Topologie d'une cité fantôme*. Paris: Minuit, 1976.

————. *Le Voyeur*. Paris: Minuit, 1955.

Robbe-Grillet, Alain, et al. "Autour du film *L'Immortelle*." *Cahiers internationaux de symbolisme* 9–10 (1966): 97–125.

Robbe-Grillet, Alain, and David Hamilton. *Les Demoiselles d'Hamilton*. Paris: Laffont, 1972.

————. *Rêves de jeunes filles*. Paris: Laffont, 1971.

Robbe-Grillet, Alain, and Irina Ionesco. *Temple aux miroirs*. Paris: Seghers-Laffont, 1977.

Robbe-Grillet, Alain, and René Magritte. *La Belle Captive*. Lausanne and Paris: La Bibliothèque des Arts, 1975.

Robbe-Grillet, Alain, and Robert Rauschenberg. *Traces suspectes en surface*. New York: Tatyana Grosman, Universal Limited Art Editions, 1978.

Roberts-Jones, Philippe. *Magritte, poète visible*. Brussels: Art du Temps / Études et Monographies, 1972.

Rybalka, Michel. Interview with Alain Robbe-Grillet. *Le Monde* 22 Sep. 1978: 7.

Saussure, Ferdinand de. *Course in General Linguistics*. New York: McGraw-Hill, 1966.

Scutenaire, Louis. *Avec Magritte*. Brussels: Lebeer-Hossman, 1977.

Simon, Claude. *La Bataille de Pharsale*. Paris: Minuit, 1969.

————. *Les Corps conducteurs*. Paris: Minuit, 1971.

Soby, James T. *René Magritte*. New York: Museum of Modern Art, 1965.

Steiner, Wendy. *The Colors of Rhetoric: Problems in the Relation Between Modern Literature and Painting*. Chicago: U of Chicago P, 1982.

————. *Pictures of Romance*. Chicago: U of Chicago P, 1992.

Stoltzfus, Ben. "Alain Robbe-Grillet and Surrealism." *Modern Language Notes* 78 (1963): 271–77.

————. *Alain Robbe-Grillet: The Body of the Text*. Madison, N.J.: Fairleigh Dickinson UP, 1985.

————. "*La Belle Captive*: Magritte and Robbe-Grillet." *Comparatist* 11 (1987): 64–75.

Sylvester, David, ed. *René Magritte, catalogue raisonné*. Vols. 1–3. Antwerp: Fonds Mercator, 1992, 1993.

Teilhard de Chardin, Pierre. *The Phenomenon of Man*. New York: Harper, 1959.

Torczyner, Harry. *Magritte: The True Art of Painting*. New York: Abrams, 1979.

Vidal, Jean-Pierre. "Remise à jour d'un polyptique insoupçonné de Magritte: *La Belle Captive*." *Obliques* 16–17 (1978): 213–24.

Vovelle, José. "René Magritte." *Le Surréalisme en Belgique*. Brussels: André de Rache, 1972. 64–164.

Waldberg, Patrick. *René Magritte*. Brussels: André De Rache, 1965.

Weisstein, Ulrich. "Literature and the Visual Arts." *Interrelations of Literature*. Ed. Jean-Pierre Barricelli and Joseph Gibaldi. New York: MLA, 1982. 251–77.

Whitfield, Sarah. *Magritte*. London: South Bank Centre, 1992.

Wittgenstein, Ludwig. *The Blue and Brown Books*. Oxford: Blackwell, 1958.

Wollheim, Richard. *Painting as an Art*. London: Thames and Hudson, 1987.

Designer: Steve Renick
Compositor: Terry Robinson & Co., Inc.
Text: 13/15 Perpetua
Display: Perpetua
Printer: Malloy Lithographing, Inc.
Binder: John H. Dekker & Sons